ONE DAY WE'LL BE HAPPY

Catherine Duke, a physiotherapist, was left a widow with three children to support when she was very young. She never dreamed that one day she might want to marry again until she met David Cullis, a successful surgeon.

But just as Catherine is about to announce her engagement to her family, things begin to go wrong. Her elder daughter, Linda, unexpectedly returns from America, obviously deeply unhappy, her son, Piers, walks out of his job and — greatest shock of all — Catherine learns that Sarah, the youngest, is seeing too much of a married man.

How can she marry David in these circumstances when her children need her guidance and care? Besides, would it be fair to him? These are the questions which torment her and which only she can answer.

Books by Renée Shann in the Ulverscroft Large Print Series:

THAT GOLDEN SUMMER
DETOUR TO DESTINY
IN TRUST TO FIONA
TIME OF THE LILAC
ONE DAY WE'LL BE HAPPY

RENÉE SHANN

ONE DAY WE'LL BE HAPPY

Complete and Unabridged

ULVERSCROFT
Leicester

First published 1972

First Large Print Edition
published June 1978

British Library CIP Data

Shann, Renee
One day we'll be happy. — Large print ed.
I. Title
823'.9'1F PR6037.H

ISBN 0-7089-0145-X

Published by
F. A. Thorpe (Publishing) Ltd.
Anstey, Leicestershire
Printed in England

Love is
a time of enchantment:
in it all days are fair and all fields
green. Youth is blest by it,
old age made benign: the eyes of love see
roses blooming in December,
and sunshine through rain. Verily
is the time of true-love
a time of enchantment — and
Oh! how eager is woman
to be bewitched!

1

THE bracket clock in the hall struck ten. A nice time, Annie thought, for them still to be having breakfast. It was unusual. Mrs. Duke was always in such a hurry to be out of the house and into her car and on her way to her patients.

In the dining-room Linda was saying to her mother, "It's wonderful to be home after this long while. I don't think I ever want to go away again."

Catherine Duke looked at her elder daughter as she sat facing her across the breakfast table. She heard the desperate note in her voice, saw the unhappiness in her eyes and wondered what had happened.

"Darling, you shan't. You've been away far too long."

"Three years, Mother."

It was the first time mother and daughter had been alone since Linda had arrived from New York the previous evening. The family had been at the airport to meet her.

They had given her a rapturous welcome. Linda, now twenty-two, the glamorous sister in her lovely American clothes, home from the States for a month's holiday. That had been what they had thought then, for Linda had said in her letters it had been all she could hope to get.

But now she was telling her mother she was here for good. Catherine asked herself why. But she didn't question Linda. She knew it would be wiser not to. Linda had always been a little withdrawn. Her mother had not been at all surprised when she had said one morning, three years ago, that she had decided to get a job in America. "I'd like to travel, Mother. Spread my wings. Besides secretaries are very well paid the other side of the Atlantic. Far better than here in England." Then, a little anxiously: "You don't mind, do you? I'll be quite all right. You'll have no need to worry about me."

Now here she was home again and Catherine knew those words spoken so confidently hadn't been true. It would seem that she had had every reason to worry about her. She wished Linda would tell her what had gone wrong.

"Sarah's grown into a real beauty, hasn't she, Mother? She was a gawky schoolgirl when I left but now — "

Catherine smiled. "She's certainly blossomed out. And doesn't she know it! She has a string of boy-friends running after her. Before we know where we are, she'll be getting married before she's really settled down into a job. She's training to be a beautician, you know, at Amanda Bruton's."

Linda laughed. "I know! She kept me awake until the early hours babbling on about the salon and the clientèle. But as regards her getting married, don't forget, Mother darling, that you married when you were very little older than Sarah is now!"

"That's true — only eighteen months. But things were different then."

"That's what the older generation always says," Linda told her. Then, pensively: "I wish I'd really known Daddy. I've only the vaguest memories of him."

"I wish you had too. You're very like him."

"In looks do you mean?"

"Yes. And in other ways too." Catherine

didn't enlarge on them. She couldn't tell Linda that, like her, her father had always been very sure of himself. Had he not been, he might have managed his affairs better and not left her with three children to bring up and very little money with which to do so.

"Piers has grown up almost out of recognition," said Linda. "Does he like this job he's doing? He's with a publisher, isn't he?"

"Yes. Lawson's. He's not very enthusiastic about it, but he's lucky to be with such a good firm. I think just now he's finding being at the bottom of the ladder rather frustrating. Officially he's a junior assistant but I gather that covers a wide field. More coffee, darling?"

"Please. Any matches about? I left my lighter in my room."

Catherine reached behind her and took a box from a side table. She wondered if Linda always smoked as much as this. Last night, when she had gone in to say goodnight to Linda after she was in bed, she had just stubbed a cigarette out in an ashtray. This morning she had been having one with her early tea.

Linda lit a cigarette and looked at her mother tentatively.

"Is it all right for me to stay here for good? I know you thought I was only coming for a holiday."

Catherine smiled at her affectionately. "What a question!"

"I thought perhaps — well, there are Piers and Sarah. I would have understood perfectly if you had been relieved to be rid of one of your children. Overjoyed, for that matter."

There was bitterness in Linda's voice and a cynicism that shouldn't have been there. Why was she saying this? Catherine wondered. What had she, her mother, ever done to make her so unfair? Then she knew it wasn't what *she* had done. Life had been responsible: it had done something harsh and cruel — and recently — so that the wound had not yet healed and she was now uncertain and unhappy, fearful of what might lie in store for her.

"From the day I saw you off at Heathrow I've been looking forward to your coming home," Catherine reassured her. "I hated your being so far away but I knew it was what you wanted."

"Mother, you're sweet."

"Don't be absurd. This is your home, darling. Where you belong."

"I've thought about it so often. Pictured you and Piers and Sarah here. Just the three of you together."

"Did you like New York?"

"For a while. But it's hectic and brash and one never seems to have time to breathe."

"London's a bit like that. It's changed a lot even in three years."

"I must see about getting a job right away."

"Wouldn't you like to take life easily for a while?"

"Oh no. Nothing would make me happier than to walk right into a job tomorrow."

There was the note of desperation in Linda's voice again, the pain in her eyes. Catherine's heart ached for her.

"In that case, you may be lucky. Though perhaps tomorrow might be rather soon. You've heard me mention Mr. Cullis in my letters — he's a well-known surgeon. He's wanting a secretary. His present one is leaving at the end of this week and the one he had engaged to take her place had an accident yesterday, so now he is urgently looking for another."

"Do you think he would take me on? I'm very efficient. Far more so than when I went to America. You need to be over there or you're out on your ear."

"I'll call him right away."

Catherine went to the telephone and returned a few minutes later to say Mr. Cullis would be glad to see Linda at half-past two.

"He's a close friend of yours, Mother, isn't he?"

"Yes. David Cullis and I have known each other a couple of years. You'll like him, I'm sure."

"I hope he'll let me start at once."

"I expect he will. You can probably start next week."

"That'll be fine. The sooner the better. I don't want to sit around doing nothing."

Because she wanted to be occupied? Catherine put out a diffident feeler. "You've lost a lot of weight in the past three years, darling. Have you been working too hard?"

"No, Mother, of course not."

"Playing too hard then?"

"It's just the pace of New York. As I said a moment ago, it's so hectic." There was an edge to Linda's voice, a warning not to pry. "You're worrying about me, Mummy, aren't you? There's no need for you to."

"I just wondered if something had happened — "

Linda leaned forward and laid a hand on her mother's arm. "Something has. A few weeks ago, but I don't want to talk about it. It's all over and I'm trying to forget it." She glanced at her watch. "Time's getting on. I'd like to get my hair washed this morning. I must make myself look my best for your Mr. Cullis."

2

CATHERINE lunched with David Cullis the following day. They discussed Linda though David didn't want to. He had seen her the previous afternoon, liked her on sight and engaged her to start work for him the following Monday. If she hadn't been Catherine's daughter, he would still have done so. She had struck him as intelligent and she would obviously make a first-class secretary. She was extremely pretty, too, he thought. She had inherited her mother's charm and it always helped to have an attractive secretary.

He wished he hadn't had the underlying feeling that she was deeply unhappy. He didn't know why he was so sure of this. It wasn't anything she had said, but there had been a look in her eyes — and he had always been good at summing people up — which had told him that, young though she was, the world had already hurt her badly.

But he didn't want to talk about her now.

He wanted to talk about Catherine and himself. To make plans for their coming marriage.

Catherine, meeting his eyes, could read his thoughts. When he had proposed to her three days ago, she had temporarily overlooked the fact that she was a widow of forty-four with three (in their opinion) grown-up children. She had been so much in love with him that she had gratefully and gladly accepted him. Now in view of Linda's return home for good and her anxiety concerning her, she wondered if she would be able to bring herself to marry David as soon as he wanted.

"Have you told your family yet, darling, that they are shortly to have a stepfather?" David asked.

"No, somehow with Linda's arrival last evening and there being so much to talk about, I've not found an opportunity."

"When will you?"

"Soon, David. This evening most likely."

"Don't delay. Surely you won't if you realise, as you must, how much I love you?"

"I don't want to. As you must know, I love you too. But— Oh, David, I've been doing some hard thinking since Linda told me yesterday morning that she had returned for good. She asked me so diffidently if she could stay. She said she knew I had only expected her for a holiday."

"But what difference does that make? Your three children will live with us. I thought I had made that perfectly clear."

"You did. At least that two of them could. But three — "

He laid a hand on Catherine's arm. "I know what's coming and I don't want to hear it."

"I'm afraid you must. Listen, you are an eligible bachelor of forty-five. I'm a middle-aged woman with three children."

"I'll grant you the three children, though I must say they seem adult to me, but you are certainly not a middle-aged woman. You're an astonishingly young one."

Catherine smiled. These were comforting words but they weren't true.

"You've not seen me early in the morning." She shook her head. "Honestly, David, I feel you should marry someone younger with no encumbrances. Someone," she hesitated, "young enough to give you children of your own."

"But I like your encumbrances. They interest me enormously. True, I hardly know Linda yet but I get on very well with the other two. As for children of my own — at my age I don't feel the need for a young family round me."

"Maybe not but I often wonder if I'm being fair to you."

"Then stop wondering. I'm the best judge of that. Tell me, which of your three is worrying you most? Or is that an unnecessary question? I've an idea it's Linda."

"You're right. She seems so withdrawn, so unhappy."

"She's probably had a broken love affair. She'll get over it."

"As you will get over it if I decide that, after all, it wouldn't be fair to marry you."

He looked at her, appalled. "Don't you believe it! For me you're a life sentence. With no remission."

Though this was true for her she couldn't help wondering if it were equally true for him. She knew he was her last love but with David there could be others. He was tall, good-looking with a lean frame and long legs. Set beneath a broad intelligent forehead the blue-grey perceptive eyes changed colour with his mood; the large mobile mouth could look either grim or sensitive. His whole appearance was one of strength and reliability. One felt one could lean on him and how Catherine longed to do just that after the years of struggle on her own. She had wondered during the past few days just when his feelings for her had developed from those of friendship to these deeper ones which had made him ask her to marry him.

They had met some eighteen months ago when his wife had been ill and Catherine had been called in by her doctor to massage her. After the wife's death he had asked Catherine once or twice to lunch with him. Then he had suggested they make it dinner. A firm friendship had developed but she had not dreamed it might become more than that. He had met her two children and heard about Linda in America. He had become a friend of the family. Though very soon she had known that, for her, if circumstances were different, he could be much more than that.

His had been a happy marriage and he had been intensely lonely when he had lost his wife but though he had taught himself to accept that loneliness the sadness hadn't lessened until recently when he had realised how much Catherine meant to him. He knew that, if only she would agree to marry him, here was a second chance of happiness. He had said, "I've been wanting to ask you to marry me for some while, but I've been almost afraid to. I've no idea how you feel about me, though surely you must know I'm in love with you."

The amazing thing was that she hadn't known. About herself she had been certain. Since it had seemed to her too much to hope for that he should fall in love with her she hadn't believed that such a miracle would happen. She had been sure that, if he remarried, he would marry someone young and beautiful. He was a successful surgeon. A catch for any woman.

"Darling, I wish I knew what to do," she said.

"You can't be serious. Damn it all, you've said you will marry me."

"I want to. But it's you I'm thinking of. And I suppose I'm also thinking of the children."

"Well, stop thinking about me and the children and think of yourself. But I warn you, I'm going to be difficult if you attempt to be a sacrificial mother."

"Aren't you being rather unreasonable?"

"Darling, no. Just realistic. And you must be too. Do you imagine your children are going to like it if they learn that because of them, you won't marry me?"

"They won't know."

"I assure you they will. And if they don't realise it for themselves I shall tell them."

"You won't if I ask you not to."

"I very likely will. I'm a determined man and I've made up my mind to marry you. As long as I'm sure you are in love with me — and I believe you are — I won't let you back out."

She felt unequal to arguing with him. Besides, she had no time. She was due at a patient in twenty minutes and, unless she left at once, she would be late.

"David, I must go. I'm sorry but I must."

He laid a detaining hand on her arm. "You'll tell the family when you have the three of them together this evening that you are going to marry me? Listen, I shall call in after dinner. You've said they will all be there. And if you haven't told them by then, I will. I warn you — " he looked at her steadily — "I mean it."

"I'll tell them." Meeting his eyes she knew that of course she would tell them. She was so deeply in love with him. And he with her. She couldn't close the door on this chance of happiness.

It was nearly seven before she was finished with her last patient. She was glad that her working day was over. Hers was an exhausting profession. Luckily, though, it was a remunerative one. It had needed to be, for bringing up three children over the years had been an expensive business.

David had said that when they married, he would prefer her not to work any more. He could comfortably be the sole breadwinner of the family. But she wouldn't want to be idle, though she wouldn't work as hard as she had in recent years. Besides, why should he be responsible for her children? Before long the older two would probably be independent. Piers already contributed a small sum each week to the housekeeping out of his salary. He had insisted that he should. And since he did so in her home, he would want to in David's. Unless, of course, he wouldn't like the idea of living with David. Though they got on well together, she thought it quite possible he might not like the idea. Once or twice recently he had hinted that he wouldn't at all mind sharing a flat with a couple of friends. If he would prefer this, a small allowance from her (which she would insist on his taking) would make it possible. Sarah would be no problem. She would probably be delighted at the prospect of David for a stepfather.

Linda was the one she would worry about. Whatever happened, Linda mustn't be allowed to go off and live on her own. Not for some while anyway. Not till this unhappiness that was haunting her had been forgotten. It must be made absolutely clear that her mother wanted Linda with her.

Catherine supposed it would all sort itself out. She couldn't bear the thought of breaking her promise to David. She couldn't bear to let this last chance of happiness slip from her.

She headed towards Wimbledon and, as

always, felt a sense of relief at leaving the West End. As she crossed Putney Bridge she thought how strange it would be to leave the pleasant though shabby little house in which she had lived for so long. She hoped Annie, without whom she would never have been able to do her job so successfully, could be persuaded to go with her. She didn't think it would be difficult: Annie was devoted to them all.

She had come to them when Catherine had been left a widow, and urgently needed to work again in order to keep her family. Without someone to run the house and look after the children this would have been impossible. She had often thought how lucky they had been when Annie had crossed their path.

She put her key in the lock. As she opened the door, Annie was crossing the hall with a laden tray on her way to the dining-room table.

"Anyone in, Annie?" she asked.

"Linda's just come back. She and Sarah are upstairs. Piers isn't home yet."

He came in as she spoke. Catherine gave him a welcoming smile but no smile answered her. She knew immediately from his expression that he was in what Sarah called one of his moods. Recently they had become increasingly frequent. She always dreaded them.

"Hallo, darling, dinner will soon be ready," she said. "It's a little late, I've only just got in. The traffic was appalling, especially over Putney Bridge."

"I don't think I want any dinner."

"That's a pity. It's one of Annie's casseroles." Catherine looked at him anxiously. "Nothing wrong, is there?"

"I expect you'll think so. I've chucked in my job. I couldn't stick it any longer."

Catherine tried to fight against a rising panic. This bombshell appalled her. She had so wanted everything to go smoothly tonight.

"Come along to my room and tell me more while I tidy."

He followed her upstairs and closed the door. She tossed her bag on the bed and hung away her coat. She was deadly tired and she wanted to wash and change and make herself look her best because this was to be such a special evening. But she couldn't with Piers standing there looking so miserable.

"I suppose you're furious," he said.

"Of course I'm not. I naturally assume you had some good reason for taking such a step. I mean . . . well, you know what you're doing."

"I know I couldn't stick that damned place any longer."

Catherine had realised that he hadn't been settling down too well at Lawson's. But she had also realised that he wouldn't make an easy employee. He was altogether too fiery. At school he hadn't been popular with his masters, or with the other pupils, except for a very few. He had always been the most difficult of her three children.

"Go ahead," he said at length, "tell me what you think of me."

"I don't know what to think. I'm sorry, of course. But I certainly wouldn't have wanted you to stay at Lawson's if you weren't happy there."

She sat down at her dressing-table and began to remove her make-up. Cleansing cream and then skin freshener, a renewed face with which to greet David, the face of a woman radiantly happy and in love, not one who was harassed and worried. But this wasn't easy to achieve.

She met Piers's angry eyes in the mirror. "Was there a row, darling?"

"Not exactly."

"Then why — ?"

"I'd rather not discuss it, Mother."

She felt a rising anger. This was all very well but it was something that surely needed discussion. More than that, it was something that should have been discussed before Piers took such a drastic step.

He moved towards the door.

"I thought I'd better tell you. I'd prefer not to make this a matter for family discussion. Linda and Sarah will have to know, but please don't let's talk about it. After all, it's my affair."

"Of course it is. But have you thought what you'll do?"

"Not yet. I only left at five o'clock this afternoon."

"Piers dear, don't take that tone with me. I'm naturally worried about you."

"I'll be all right."

Linda's cry. And look what had happened to Linda!

They heard Annie calling up the stairs that dinner was ready.

"I'll go and clean up," said Piers. "You

won't mind if I clear out after dinner, will you? I don't feel like sitting at home this evening."

"Of course not, but I'd rather you were here. David Cullis is coming in later."

"I don't need to be in for him, do I?"

"Not if you don't want to, though I'd like you to be."

No answer. The door closed behind Piers. She heard him cross the landing and his bedroom door slam. She pictured him in his room, looking morosely out of his window, his shoulders hunched, his head lowered — a characteristic attitude.

If only he would confide in her, give her some hint as to what had gone wrong at Lawson's. But he obviously didn't propose to. Just as Linda didn't propose to tell her what had happened in New York.

She heard Linda and Sarah going downstairs, Sarah chatting volubly. Sarah was the easiest of her children. Her worst fault was that she was inclined to be headstrong and always anxious to get her own way.

Sarah called out now that dinner was on the table. Catherine gave a last glance at herself in the mirror. Despite her efforts she wasn't looking her best.

The two girls were sitting at the table when she entered the room.

"Had a tiring day, Mother?" asked Linda.

"Fairly."

"You look a bit weary."

Catherine sighed inwardly. This wasn't at all the way she wanted to look.

"Mr. Cullis is coming round after dinner," she told them.

Linda's face lit up. "That's good. I thought he was terribly nice when I saw him yesterday."

"He's dishy," said Sarah. "Maybe he'll fall for you, Linda. Or would he be too old? How old is he, Mother?"

"Forty-five."

"Just right."

Catherine's heart missed a beat. What were the girls going to think when they learned it was their mother he wanted to marry?

"Mind if I start, Mummy?" said Sarah. "I'm in a hurry. I've got a date after dinner."

The celebration party, it would seem, was dwindling. Catherine knew, if she was to give her children the news as she had promised David, she had better not delay. She wished she didn't feel so reluctant to tell them. It wasn't only their personal reactions she flinched from. She felt now a lurking embarrassment. Apparently it hadn't occurred to them that she might one day want to marry again. Certainly not to Sarah.

"An important date, Sarah?"

"Only Harriet. There's a Western on at the local we want to see."

"Shall I call Piers?" said Linda. "His dinner will be cold if he's much longer."

"I don't suppose he'll be a minute. Hungry, darling?"

"Not very."

"I am," said Sarah. "I'm starving."

"Aren't you afraid of putting on weight?" asked her sister. "You should see the way girls of your age diet in America."

"Actually I have got fatter lately. But only in the right places. That reminds me, Mummy, I was looking at one of the women's mags today. There was an article on how to avoid a middle-aged spread. I nearly bought it for you."

"Thanks very much," said Catherine drily.

Linda laughed. "Mother's still got a marvellous figure."

"I know. But she needs to be careful."

Catherine wondered how she could possibly tell her family her news. It was growing more and more difficult. Now Piers, looking pale and drawn, entered the room. He sat down without a word.

"What's wrong with you?" asked Sarah.

Piers glowered at her. "Nothing."

"Have some more, Sarah," said Catherine quickly.

"No, thank you. Must we wait for Piers? Couldn't we have the pudding right away?"

"Don't let me keep any of you," said Piers.

"That's all right, darling, there's no hurry."

"There is, Mummy. At least for me," said Sarah. "I told you. I'm meeting Harriet."

Catherine decided that it was time she was firm with her family.

"I don't want any of you rushing off this evening. In fact, I'd prefer it, Sarah, if you would phone Harriet and tell her you'll meet her another night. That film can wait. I particularly wanted you all at home."

"Why?"

"I'll tell you when we've finished dinner."

Would she? Would she even now find it impossible to keep her promise to David? In which case she would have to meet him at the door when he arrived and tell him she had let him down. But she wanted to keep her promise so desperately. She began to form little sentences in her mind. "Darlings, I've some news for you. Linda, Piers, Sarah — "

The telephone bell rang. Sarah pushed back her chair to fly to answer it. But Annie forestalled her.

"It's for your mother," she said as Sarah went out to the hall.

"Someone for you, Mother," Sarah called.

Catherine closed the dining-room door, expecting it to be a patient arranging an appointment.

"Who is that? This is Mrs. Duke speaking."

A rather uncertain voice apologised for disturbing her. "You don't know me. My name's Mrs. Gold."

"Oh, yes?"

There was a pause. Mrs. Gold seemed singularly hesitant in explaining why she was telephoning.

"Is it about a massage?" asked Catherine.

"No. It's about your daughter." And then, the unknown voice sharper: "Mrs. Duke, would you please stop her from going out with my husband?"

Catherine was appalled. Her hand tightened round the telephone receiver. This was the last thing she had expected to hear. But it explained why Linda was looking so unhappy. This was why she had come rushing home. But she had come rushing home from New York and Mrs. Gold was surely making a local call? Still this meant nothing. Perhaps Linda and the husband had met in the States and returned together? Perhaps his wife had only now found out about her? Catherine had realised there was a man responsible for Linda's misery. She had guessed, too, that he was probably married.

"It's ruining my life," went on Mrs. Gold. "We were happy before he met her. But now . . ."

Catherine was at a loss to know what to

say. How did a mother cope with such a situation?

"I'm most terribly sorry. Yes, I'll certainly do what I can. I had no idea — "

"I thought you couldn't have. That's why I'm calling you. That and because I can't stand it any longer. I know she's very young . . ."

"Linda's twenty-two," Catherine said gently. "And very adult."

"Linda? Her name's not Linda. It's Sarah."

Catherine leaned against the wall, shocked at this unexpected disclosure.

"She's meeting him again tonight, I know."

Sarah, thought Catherine. Sarah whom she had believed to be her easiest child, the child about whom she had least cause to worry.

"I'll stop it at once, Mrs. Gold. I thought at first you meant my elder daughter."

"No, I didn't know you had another one. I'm sorry if I've upset you."

Catherine put down the telephone. She stood for a moment too shocked to move. Then she forced herself to return to the dining-room, to talk and behave as if nothing had happened. Because she couldn't tackle Sarah about it this evening, not till David had come and gone anyway.

"Why do you particularly want me at home this evening, Mummy?" Sarah wanted to know.

"Because I do," said Catherine, falling back on that old answer of adults which she had always tried not to use because she knew it was infuriating to the young.

Sarah pouted. "But I've promised Harriet — "

"As I've already told you, you can phone her and say I want you at home."

"Anyone would think I was a child."

Catherine ignored this. She glanced at Linda and Piers. Both of them seemed to be eating scarcely anything.

"If you're all finished we'll go into the drawing-room," she said.

Still she hadn't told them. And now, after that telephone call, how could she? She had believed it was Linda who needed her most, that she had had no need to worry about the other two. Now she felt too distracted to consider herself and David.

Before she had realised it, he was in the

room. Sarah had seen him coming to the house from the window and had hurried to let him in. He shook hands with Linda and said he was glad to see her again and how much he was looking forward to her working for him.

"I'm looking forward to coming."

Piers edged towards the door. "You don't mind if I go, do you, Mother? Please don't think me rude, David, but there's something I must see to."

"Wait a few minutes, Piers," said Catherine.

David glanced at them all. Then he looked at Catherine.

"Haven't you told them our news, Catherine?"

"I was just going to." She smiled hesitantly. "I think you'd better tell them, David."

Linda, Piers and Sarah looked at him expectantly.

"I hope you'll all be pleased. Your mother and I are going to be married."

Catherine knew that for ever afterwards the expression on her children's faces would be photographed on her mind. Linda's was at first delighted then anxiety swiftly followed. Piers's lips compressed and his eyes were puzzled. Sarah was clearly completely astounded.

Piers seemed to realise he should say something. He kissed his mother, said he was delighted and held out his hand to David.

"Congratulations."

"Thank you."

Linda, too, kissed her mother. "Mother darling, this is marvellous," she said but her tone was flat and Catherine knew she was making a tremendous effort.

"I'm terribly glad, Mr. Cullis. I realise we've only just met but I am sure Mother's going to be very happy and, if I may say so, you are too."

"I know I am, Linda," said David confidently.

Sarah flung her arms round Catherine's neck and said it was wonderful news but so utterly astonishing.

"Why, Sarah?"

"Well, Mummy . . ."

Catherine laughed. "You think I'm too old to marry again?"

"No, of course not," said Sarah far too emphatically.

Catherine turned to Piers. "Darling, could you find some drinks?"

"Yes, of course."

Piers fetched them from the dining-room cupboard.

"Whisky, David?"

"Please."

"Mother?"

"A very weak one."

"It should be champagne," said Sarah.

"It will be next time," David said. "I suggest you all have dinner with me tomorrow night to celebrate."

Piers handed glasses to Linda and Sarah and gave a rather forced smile.

"To you both," he said to his mother and David.

"To us all," said David. "When your mother and I are married I want the three of you to make your home with us."

"Super," said Sarah and hugged David.

The other two murmured their thanks, but Catherine knew neither liked the idea.

Piers sat down with his empty glass. "If you'll both forgive me, I have letters I must write."

Sarah glanced at the clock. "Mummy, you don't mind if I go off and meet

Harriet, do you? I'm terribly late as it is. And I can't call her and put her off. She'll have left home by now."

Catherine held out her hand to her. "If you're not there she'll think, quite rightly, that something has detained you."

But Sarah slipped from the room before Catherine could stop her. Now Linda, with a smile to her mother and David, said she hoped they would excuse her but she too, had letters to write.

David waited till the door closed behind her. Then he went to Catherine and took her in his arms and kissed her. "Your children obviously think we want to be left alone. As we do, don't we, darling?" He drew her down beside him on the sofa. "Why hadn't you told them, Catherine?"

"I hadn't an opportunity. And things have been happening."

"I guessed that. But let me tell you that, whatever they are, nothing is going to make any difference. Just get that firmly fixed in your head and then tell me what is worrying you."

Catherine sighed. "Quite a lot."

"Piers?"

"Yes."

"Sarah, too?"

"Yes."

"That's two of them and I know you are anxious about Linda. What have Piers and Sarah been up to? I'm here to help and advise you."

Catherine leaned her head against his shoulder. She thought how lucky she was to have David in love with her and wanting to marry her. If only things were straightforward! Plenty of widows of her age with grown-up children remarried. They were entitled to. No woman of forty-four or even older wanted to go through life alone. She had been alone long enough to realise how empty life was, how pointless, without a partner. It wasn't living, it was existing. And it would grow more lonely as the years passed. The children would one day marry. They might need her now but not always. If she let this chance of happiness pass her by, then what would become of her? Some women she knew were content to live alone but she wasn't one of them.

"Piers has left Lawson's."

"That's a silly thing to do. Why?"

"He hasn't told me. He just said he

couldn't stick the damned place any longer."

"Probably there was a row. Maybe it can be put right."

"It doesn't sound like it. I know Piers."

"What about Sarah?"

"I had a telephone call at dinner."

"On the many occasions I've dined with you you've had telephone calls at dinner."

"I know, but this was from a woman who asked me to stop my daughter going out with her husband."

David looked at her, appalled. "That's certainly serious."

"Very. I thought at first it must be Linda she was referring to, but it was Sarah."

"Good God! How old is she?"

"Seventeen. It's shattering. And just before dinner I was thinking she was the one I had no need to worry about." Catherine shook her head wearily. "I love you, David, and I want to marry you, but in view of all this, how can I?"

His arm tightened round her shoulders and he smoothed her furrowed brow with gentle fingers. He felt infinitely sorry for her but he was determined not to let her go back on her promise. And for the moment he wasn't thinking of himself. He was thinking of Catherine. She deserved to be happy. He knew what a struggle she had had to bring up her family, how hard she had worked. He longed to take care of her and make life easier for her.

"We'll sort it out," he promised. "The important thing is that you *are* going to marry me. And soon if I have any say in the matter."

"But, darling, put yourself in my place. Would you marry me if you had so many responsibilities? These are my children and I've got to cope with them. And if I'm coping with them, how can I be a happy wife and hope to make you happy?"

He said gently, "You're over-tired this evening. You can't see the wood for the trees. But it will be all right. We'll put our heads together and solve all three problems. But not tonight. Look, I'm going to give myself another drink and give you one too and then I'll be on my way. You get some rest. We'll lunch together as usual tomorrow and see what can be done about everything."

3

SARAH raced down the road and reached the bus stop quite out of breath. She looked anxiously up and down. Garry was nowhere to be seen. Had he grown tired of waiting for her? She was twenty minutes late but surely he must have known she would arrive eventually?

She had never broken a date with him yet and she was never going to. Though what would happen if her mother found out about these constant meetings she dared not think. Her mother would disapprove strongly because he was a married man. She wouldn't understand that his wife was impossible to live with, that they had never got on and he had made a great mistake in marrying her.

She tapped her foot impatiently wondering why he was keeping her waiting. Then she saw him coming towards her, and ran to meet him, her face radiant, her eyes shining.

He held her close and kissed her.

"Darling, I've been looking everywhere for you," she said.

"I like that! I was beginning to think you were never coming. I just nipped into that bar over there to have a quick one." He held her at arm's length. "Is it really only twenty-four hours since I last saw you? I'd forgotten how lovely you were."

Sarah felt a surge of happiness. Garry said such marvellous things. Every time she saw him she fell more deeply in love with him.

"Where shall we go, darling?" he asked. "A cinema or a walk on the common?"

"Let's go on the common."

They set off together, her arm through his, his hand holding hers.

"I'm afraid I can't be out terribly long," she said. "I must be in by the time the cinema would be over. Mummy believes I'm there with Harriet."

"OK. I'll keep my eye on the time."

"What do you think's happened at home?"

"I've no idea."

"Mummy's going to marry again. I was absolutely staggered."

Garry chuckled. "Why? She's not all that old, is she?"

"I suppose not really. But — I don't know — somehow I never dreamed anyone would want to marry her. I suppose it's because she's my mother."

"I hope you didn't sound too astonished when she told you. It can't have been very flattering. I thought you said she was in her early forties."

"So she is."

"Well, that's not old."

"It seems so to me. I suppose that's because she's my mother."

"Let me remind you that I'm in my thirties."

"That's different."

Garry dropped a light kiss on her forehead and his hold on her hand tightened. "Darling, you are a little comic."

Sarah pouted. She didn't like it when Garry took this line with her. As if she were a baby.

"But you're adorable," he went on, realising he had put his foot in it.

Sarah gave a blissful sigh. "Oh, Garry! It's heaven to be with you."

They were reaching a quiet part of the

common. They had a special place which they had made their own. Nobody else seemed to have discovered it. The trees were tall and gave them shelter and they could be undisturbed. Other couples were doubtless not far away but this was their special haven.

It was growing dark now. The last faint streaks of sunset were fading in the western sky. Sarah lay on the soft grass, Garry's arms encircling her. She wished her conscience didn't choose such inconvenient moments to smite her. After all, she was doing no harm. True, she let Garry kiss her perhaps more passionately than was wise. But she knew she could trust him. She could not withhold a small sigh. She wished she could tell her mother. She didn't like deceiving her.

"Why the sigh?" asked Garry.

"I don't know. It just escaped me."

Garry smoothed her hair back from her forehead. "Sometimes I wonder if I should see so much of you."

Sarah leaned on her elbow and looked up at him, a shiver of fear running through her.

"Why do you say that, darling?"

"I'm married — "

"As if I care."

"But *I* should."

"Why? You told me you didn't get on with your wife. That you never have."

It was Garry's turn to sigh. Sarah was so naïve. She believed so trustingly everything he said to her. Not that this wasn't true though he doubted if his wife, Emma, would agree that they didn't get on. At first they had been rapturously happy. But they had married so young and as the years had passed they had drifted apart. He knew this was very much his fault. He doubted if he could make any woman lastingly happy.

"I know, Sarah, but when you are older you will discover that all married men who run around with single girls assure them that they aren't happy with their wives."

The fear in Sarah's heart deepened. Was Garry trying to warn her that he wasn't as deeply in love with her as she believed? Surely he couldn't be?

"Why are you talking to me like this? I thought your wife didn't matter to you any more or you to her. You said last time we were together you were going to get a divorce."

Garry cursed himself for having been

such a fool. He supposed if Emma and he continued to live their present cat and dog life, a divorce would be their only solution. He forgot that he had told Sarah this was in his mind. He remembered that he had had far more drinks that night than had been wise. He'd brought off a double on the horses and he had been celebrating with some pals before he had met her.

"Maybe we will."

"Only maybe?"

"Sarah — please — don't try to get me in a corner."

"I'm sorry. But you did say so." And fearfully: "You aren't trying to tell me that you're not going to after all?" Sarah's lips trembled. "Garry, darling, please tell me you're not."

"Of course I'm not," he said, despising himself for being so weak with her. But he couldn't bear to hurt her. She was so enchanting and, yes, he supposed he was in love with her, but he was by no means sure that, even if he were no longer married to Emma, he would want to spend the rest of his days with Sarah. That was the worst of women. Even young ones like Sarah. They always wanted to tie a man down. To insist on his making protestations and promises that, if they had any sense, they would realise he would be unable to keep.

He bent his head and kissed her, knowing this was one way to stop further questioning. He thought how attractive she was and how infinitely desirable. He wished she were more like the other girls he had imagined himself in love with over the past years since he had begun to find life so impossible with Emma. Girls who had come from a different walk of life, who hadn't been brought up with such a strict code of right and wrong. For he knew from what Sarah had told him that, if he overstepped the mark, he would be heading for serious trouble. This might be a permissive society but Sarah didn't belong to it, which he found surprising because most girls did.

He touched her hair with his lips.

"Feeling happier now?"

"Much. Kiss me again, Garry. The way you did just now."

Garry did so willingly. He held her more closely, aware of the rising emotion stirring within her. She was made for love, he thought, but was he being fair to her. He was finding it damned hard to keep his self-made promise that, in no circumstances, would he allow his own emotion to run riot and so ultimately cause her distress. That he had violated her moral code in persuading her to continue to meet him once she knew he was already married did, on occasion, cause him some uneasiness. On the other hand, at times she appeared to be purposely provocative.

"Did you say you wanted to be in by eleven?" he asked as a clock struck in the distance.

"Darling, don't remind me."

"I don't want to. But just occasionally my better nature gets the better of me."

"I wish it wouldn't."

Garry thought how hard she was making it for him. But he supposed she didn't realise the strain she was putting him to.

"You're a wicked one, aren't you, Sarah?"

"I'm a loving one."

Garry got up, held out his hands and dragged her to her feet.

"Turn round," he said and he brushed the tell-tale blades of dried grass from her skirt. "There, that's better."

Sarah giggled. "You think of everything, don't you?"

"Well, you needed a bit of tidying up."

They strolled back across the common. The stars were shining brilliantly, the trees etched in sharp relief against the blue-black sky.

"I love the common," said Sarah softly. "I'd hate to live right in London." She wondered where they would live when her mother married. David had a large flat near Regent's Park. There would be plenty of room for them all but it wouldn't be the same. Perhaps he would find somewhere else for his new-found family. She supposed this was quite likely. He could afford to. Apparently he was very successful and made a great deal of money.

Garry said firmly, "Unless you're looking for trouble, you must hurry home now like a good little girl."

"I know. I wonder if my future step-father will still be there?"

"Who is he, by the way?"

"A Mr. Cullis. He's a successful surgeon and terribly nice. I thought he might have done for Linda."

"I hope you didn't tell your mother so."

"I did more or less."

"That wasn't very tactful of you."

Sarah leaned her head against Garry's shoulder. "If I marry you and I am left a widow, I'll never marry again."

Oh God, thought Garry, why had Sarah such a one-track mind this evening? He didn't at all like this talk of marriage. He wished he hadn't been such a fool as to suggest he had ever considered it.

As they reached the corner of her road they stopped. Sarah turned to Garry and he held her to him closely. He never went any nearer to the house. It was too risky. Someone might see them. They kissed good-night in their usual sheltered little corner.

"I'm not sure about tomorrow but if I can make it, I will," he said. "Anyway, phone me."

He never telephoned her but left it for her to ring him at the office. It would arouse suspicion if he rang her.

"Actually I can't manage tomorrow. My future stepfather is taking us all out to dinner."

"Monday night then. Same place, same time."

He kissed her again and this time she

managed to drag herself away. She hurried up the road and paused outside the gate leading to the house. She put a hand up to her hair to smooth it into place. She wished it wasn't so dark. She would like to look in her compact to reassure herself that her eyes weren't shining too brightly, that she didn't look like a girl who had just been kissed.

She slid her key quietly in the lock. There was a light beneath the drawing-room door. As her mother usually went to bed early, she hoped this meant that David was still there. In which case she could call out good-night and go quietly upstairs without disturbing them.

"That you, Sarah?"

She halted at the sound of her mother's voice. The next moment the drawing-room door opened.

"Come in a minute, darling," said Catherine, "I want to talk to you."

Sarah guessed what was coming. Her mother was about to reassure her in case she wasn't happy at the idea of her marrying David. She was going to point out that it would make no difference to them as a family.

"Sit down, Sarah," said Catherine. "You remember I had a phone call during dinner?"

Sarah had forgotten it. The walk on the common with Garry had put all else from her mind. Now it came back to her and with it a sharp awareness that everything wasn't going the way she had expected. Her mother looked somehow hurt and worried.

"I remember."

"It was from a Mrs. Gold. She asked me to stop you going out with her husband."

Sarah's heart gave a sudden lurch. This was the last thing she had expected, but she was determined to stand up to it.

"Oh, she did, did she?"

"Why have you been lying to me, Sarah? It's not like you. At least I would have hoped not."

Catherine watched Sarah closely as she was speaking. She had seen the child's face lose colour. She felt a sudden heartbreaking pity for her. She was so young, so vulnerable. And she, her mother, was so desperately anxious to handle her the right way. Whatever happened she mustn't antagonise her.

"I'm sorry, Mummy," said Sarah. "But how could I tell you?"

Catherine's eyes darkened with pain. Why couldn't Sarah have told her? Because she had felt she couldn't confide in her? It couldn't be that surely? But she knew that at her age she couldn't have confided in her mother. But times had changed since she was a girl. Many mothers were more like sisters to their daughters. It would seem that she wasn't one of them. And she wondered if it was because she had always been working so hard and therefore hadn't been able to keep as close an eye on Sarah as she should have done. If she had been a stay-at-home mother with only her children to consider would this dilemma not have happened?

Sarah was recovering from the first shock. Her head lifted. She met her mother's eyes defiantly.

"You can't stop me seeing Garry, Mummy. Whatever his wife says, you can't stop me."

Catherine hesitated. "You think you're in love with him?"

She wished instantly she could withdraw these words. She mustn't suggest that

Sarah was too young to be in love, that she couldn't be expected to know that she could be infatuated with a man but a day would come when she would find he no longer mattered to her.

"I am in love with him. And he's in love with me."

"How old is he?"

"In the early thirties."

"And he knows your age?"

Sarah hesitated. Actually she had told Garry she was twenty when she had first met him at a party. She had not wanted to admit to being only seventeen. And that night she had had a new hair-style and had been wearing a maxi-dress. In her opinion she believed she could have said she was over twenty-one and got away with it. Still one day when the divorce was through and they were about to be married, she would have to tell him that she had lived three years less in the world. She sighed inwardly. She hated lying to her mother. It was awful having a conscience even if only a small one.

"What does he do, darling?"

"He's a PRO. A very successful one. He's quite a catch really."

"Except that he has a wife."

"They're going to be divorced."

Catherine could hardly bear the confidence in Sarah's voice. How gullible she was! In some ways she was younger than her seventeen years, almost a child.

"That's not what Mrs. Gold gave me to understand. In fact, she said they had been ideally happy till he met you."

"That's not true. They've never been happy. Garry says their marriage was a mistake from the outset. She's led him an awful life. I don't believe she's even been faithful to him."

"Did he tell you that?"

"Yes."

"It didn't occur to you that there could be two sides to every story? Anyway, it wasn't a nice way for a husband to talk about his wife even if it was true."

Sarah had thought this herself, but she hadn't let it concern her.

Catherine said gently, "Darling, I don't like the sound of it."

"I don't expect you do."

"I'd like to ask you not to see him again."

"It wouldn't be any use."

Catherine knew she was up against a brick wall. Sarah was self-willed and stubborn. All her children were but Sarah even more than the others. Maybe all children liked to have their own way — children at least with any character. And hers, she fondly believed, had a great deal of character. She wished she knew what line to take. Tomorrow David would doubtless advise her and his advice would be sound and if she had any sense she would take it. All the same it was a difficult situation. If she were to insist that Sarah stopped seeing this man, she might only throw her more precipitously into his arms. The best thing might be to see him herself.

Sarah said, "The divorce will be one of those arranged ones. Many of them are."

Catherine drew a deep breath. This from her seventeen-year-old! She held out her hand to Sarah. "Maybe, darling, but I'm terribly worried."

Sarah said brokenly, "I'm sorry, Mummy. I hate you to be. But — well, Garry . . ."

"Garry . . ." prompted Catherine.

"I don't know how to put it." And then in a little embarrassed rush, her cheeks flaming; "I mean he doesn't want to pop into bed with me." And defiantly, "Whatever you say, I won't stop seeing him."

Catherine drew her rebellious young daughter to her and kissed her.

"All right, darling, we'll say no more about it tonight. Let's go to bed. You must be tired and heaven knows I am!"

It was only after she had locked the front door that she paused to wonder if her other two children were safely in bed. She crept into Linda's room and found her reading. She stooped and kissed her.

"Good-night, darling."

"Good-night, Mother."

As she closed the door, Catherine wished Linda had said one little word about the news of her marriage to David. She wondered whether to go back to reassure Linda that, when she married David, their home would be her home just as much as this one was her home. But it might be wiser not to.

She paused outside Piers's door. She rarely disturbed him once he went to bed. But tonight she felt so anxious. She opened his door quietly. The curtains were not drawn and the moonlight shining through the window showed her that the bed was empty. Her heart sank. What was he doing? Walking alone on the common, head bent, his hands dug deep in his pockets, thinking, thinking, thinking? Rebelling against this world in which he felt he had no part?

She closed his door and went downstairs to unlock the front door. Sarah, on her way from the bathroom, looking about fourteen in her childish dressing-gown, saw her mother coming upstairs and felt a sudden pang at her white drawn face. She thought suddenly that it wasn't fair she should be looking like this and that Linda, Piers and she were to blame. This should have been a very special evening. It was staggering, of course, that her mother was going to marry David but it was exciting and they should all be rejoicing. It was wrong that they were so concerned with their own problems that they couldn't put them aside and think only of her. For this one night at least. She held up her face for a good-night kiss.

"Good-night, Mummy. I wish we weren't all such a nuisance to you. Especially now when you should be so happy."

Catherine put an arm round her

shoulders. "You're not a nuisance. I just get anxious about you sometimes."

"Oh yes, we are. Something's wrong with Piers, that's obvious. Goodness knows what's the matter with Linda. And I'm running around with a married man. I'll tell you this," she said, her voice full of purpose, "when I marry Garry I won't have any children."

4

LINDA put the car into neutral and resigned herself to yet another traffic jam. She wondered if the traffic in London could be even worse than in New York. There seemed little to choose between Fifth Avenue and Piccadilly.

At last it moved on again. She turned down Knightsbridge and into Hans Crescent, stopping outside the block of flats where she had promised to call for her mother. She glanced at her watch. Seven o'clock. Despite the traffic it was pretty good timing. Her mother had said she would be through by then. As she drew in to the kerb, a tall grey-haired man came towards her.

"Miss Duke? I'm Rupert Morrison. Your mother is just having a drink. Won't you come in and have one too? We would so much like it."

He was holding the car door open as he spoke. Though Linda longed to refuse, she knew it would be discourteous. But she hated meeting new people. She thought in sharp irritation that her mother might have spared her this. She must know she wasn't feeling sociable.

Reluctantly she got out of the car and followed her host into the lift.

"We have a young American here this evening," he said as he ushered her into his flat on the top floor. "He only flew in this afternoon. You must meet him."

Linda almost turned and went straight out again. But she knew that would have been ridiculous. In the course of her life she would have to meet many young Americans.

"Ah, darling, here you are. Mrs. Morrison, this is my daughter." Catherine drew Linda towards her.

Linda shook hands with her hostess and found that she was involved in a cocktail party. More than ever she wished her mother had saved her from it.

She laid her hand on her mother's arm. "We can't stay long, Mother. The car isn't parked too well. I saw a traffic warden with his eyes on it."

Mrs. Morrison laughed this aside, and assured Linda that cars could be left without worrying unduly. Hadn't Linda noticed that there were a number outside already?"

"Were there? I suppose I just wasn't looking."

Mr. Morrison broke in on them. "Miss Duke, what can I give you to drink? A dry Martini or a sherry?"

"A sherry, please."

"Dirk," Mr. Morrison said to a tall, good-looking young man at his side, "I don't think you have met Miss Duke. Miss Duke, this is Dirk Marion."

"Your mother tells me you are just back from the States," said Dirk Marion.

"Yes."

"I flew in today. Did you like it over there?"

"Fairly well," said Linda, experience having taught her that Americans were inclined to be touchy about their country.

"Where were you?"

"In New York mostly, though once or twice I went up to Connecticut."

"You should have gone south."

"So I was told."

The other guests had drawn away from them and they were isolated in the way two people could be isolated in a crowded room with chatter going on around them. Linda looked over at her mother, who was now chatting to Mr. and Mrs. Morrison, and wished she could catch her eye. She wanted to get away. But though her mother glanced across at her and smiled, she turned back to her host and hostess.

"Were you in the States long?" asked Dirk Marion.

Linda took a tight hold of herself. She reminded herself that he was only making polite conversation. They were a man and a girl meeting at a cocktail party. It was expected of him to make himself pleasant to her. Only she wished he had chosen something other than America to talk about.

"Yes. For three years I had a job out there. Are you going to be in England long?"

This, she thought, should turn the tables. Let him talk about England. This was her home ground. She could talk about it contentedly. She was fond of England. It was a beautiful country and she didn't even mind the climate.

"Quite a while. I'm with an oil firm over here."

"Have you been here before?"

"No, but I've always wanted to come. Tell me, where did you live in New York?"

"East twenty-fifth Street." And then to be free of him even if only for a moment: "Would you get me another drink? A soft one this time. I'm driving."

He was back sooner than she wanted.

"Strange you should have returned so recently from my home country," he said. "I've friends in East twenty-fifth Street. I know Up Town's classier but I prefer the Village and I love Washington Square."

Washington Square. Linda hated being reminded of it. The trees at night with the moon shining down on them. Eighth Street with its medley of narrow streets thronging with artists and happy-go-lucky people, many of them with very little money. The restaurants where they so often dined. There had been one in particular that was their favourite. They always had the same Italian waiter. One night as they were leaving, he smiled at them. She could see him again. Hear his voice. "You are the happiest couple I have ever served on." Oh God, she prayed, don't let me remember! Please don't let me remember!

"D'you know," said Dirk Marion, "I've an idea I've met you before. You weren't by any chance living in that block of apartments at the far end of twenty-fifth Street? My friends have one on the eighteenth floor. Their name's Clifton. Perhaps you know them?"

"I don't. I was the other end of the street." She forced herself to smile. "There are a lot of people living in it."

"I know. It's just that your face seems familiar."

Linda longed to escape. She had lived in that very block. And her face must be familiar because Dirk Marion had seen it in the papers. Hank and she had been front-page news for a brief twenty-four hours. Only, thank God, sensation was so commonplace in the States that it was swiftly forgotten, swiftly overtaken by another sensational piece of drama. But could Dirk Marion be remembering who she was and was he questioning her to make sure?

Thankfully she saw her mother coming towards her.

"Ready, darling? If so, we'll go."

"Quite ready, Mother."

"Mr. Marion, do come and have a drink

one evening," said Catherine, who had been told by Mrs. Morrison that the young American knew nobody as yet in London and she would like him to meet some young people. "We live out at Wimbledon. I have a son and another daughter." She gave him their address and telephone number. "One night next week?"

"Thanks a lot. I'll be delighted."

Catherine consulted the little engagement book she always carried in her bag. "How about next Wednesday?"

"That'll be fine."

"About seven then. I can't make it any earlier because I'm a career woman and I don't get in till around then."

"I'll probably be later," said Linda. "I never know how long Mr. Cullis will keep me."

"You'll be home by then easily, darling," said Catherine.

Dirk held out his hand to Linda. "Till Wednesday then. I'll look forward to seeing you again."

Catherine was aware that Linda interested him and was glad she had asked him. And though Linda apparently hadn't liked America she couldn't be so insular as to suggest there were no pleasant Americans. It would do her good to meet some nice ones, she thought, as she too said good-bye to Dirk. He might make her change her opinion of his fellow countrymen.

She was, therefore, quite taken aback by Linda's bitter tone as they drove away from Hans Crescent.

"Did you have to ask Dirk Marion out to see us, Mother?"

"But, darling, why shouldn't I? I thought he was charming."

"Did you?"

"Didn't you?"

"Not particularly. You won't mind if I'm not in next Wednesday? I loathe cocktail parties."

"I wasn't proposing that we would have a cocktail party. But Mrs. Morrison says, as yet, he knows no young people over here and it seemed only friendly to invite him."

"Well, let Piers and Sarah entertain him."

Catherine sighed. She was tired after a long day's work. She wished Linda wasn't taking this line over Dirk Marion.

"I'd like you to be there, too, darling."

Linda didn't answer. She was feeling too

upset and ill. To think that she had walked into some unexpected cocktail party and found herself forced to talk to a man who had lived in the same block! Who had forced her to remember when all she longed for was to forget.

Catherine, glancing at Linda's set, white face, was shocked at her look of stark suffering. Here was the old Linda who could be mulish when she chose, who shut up like a clam so that even she, her mother, daren't try to get through to her.

"Of course you don't have to be in if you'd rather not."

"I'll see how I feel when Wednesday comes." And then, realising that she was behaving badly, remembering that at the end of the day her mother was doubtless feeling more than usually tired, "I'm sorry, Mother. I don't want to be horrid. It's just that all I want is to be left alone. And, please, if your idea is to find young men to amuse me, I'd much rather you didn't."

5

"PHONE, Piers," called Annie.

It was an evening a week later. Piers put down the book he was reading and went reluctantly to answer.

He picked up the receiver. "Hallo," he said warily.

"Hallo, Piers. Jane here."

As if he hadn't known it would be! Jane was Mr. Lawson's secretary. They had met the first day he had joined the firm. She was a year younger than he and she also had literary aspirations. She had far more chance of achieving them, Piers knew, than he had. For one thing, she wasn't afraid of hard work and rejection slips never intimidated her. She just assumed they were part and parcel of the training to be an author.

They had quarrelled bitterly the day he had decided to leave Lawson's. He had told her he was doing so when they lunched together at their usual cheap little restaurant and she had tried to dissuade him. The biting things she had said to him when he said his mind was made up still rankled.

He supposed now she was regretting that she hadn't behaved rather differently because they had seen a great deal of each other while he had worked for the firm. Each day they had lunched together and often they would go to a cinema or out for a meal in the evenings.

"I wondered how you were getting on?" she said, her voice surprisingly wistful and docile, very different from the way it had been when last they had met.

"I'm OK."

"What have you been doing?"

"Nothing particular."

"Oh, Piers!"

"I've told you, Jane, and I tell you again, I'm a born idler."

"Then you've no business to be. Anyway, I don't believe you."

"Suppose you tell me what you've been doing? Out of office hours, that is. Not that you need to. Writing like a potential Jane Austen, I suppose, whenever you have a spare minute." There was a biting sarcasm in his voice but he didn't care.

"Piers dear, don't be so bad-tempered,"

she said, which made him even more exasperated.

There was a pause. "I can't think why I bother with you," she said.

"I can't either."

"It could be that I'm fond of you."

"In which case you should have more sense."

"I dare say. Listen, this is getting us nowhere. I don't suppose you would like to see me?"

Piers wasn't sure. There had been times since he had left Lawson's when he had been astonished to find how much he longed to see Jane. But now that she was there at the other end of the line, he was undecided. He didn't want to have another row with her. The last one had been too painful.

"Don't if you'd rather not," she said. "But I'll be lunching in our usual little restaurant at the usual time tomorrow and I'll be on the look-out for you."

As he replaced the receiver, Piers told himself that she would look in vain. He'd be damned if he would be there. But, very much to his surprise, he found himself sauntering into the restaurant next day at lunchtime and looking round to see if she were there already.

Jane, who had been waiting a good ten minutes hoping he would come, one moment telling herself that he wasn't likely to, the next that surely he must, saw him and waved.

"I've been saving a seat for you," she said as he joined her. "It wasn't easy. They're very full today."

The waitress stood at Piers's elbow. "Have you ordered?" he asked Jane.

"I've already started. Have the fried fish. It's good."

Piers ordered it, said he wasn't hungry but supposed he had better have something. And as the girl left them: "Well, here I am. Fire ahead. Tell me what you think of me."

"I'm not sure that would be wise."

"I'd say it would be most unwise."

"I'll tell you instead that it's very good to see you."

"Thanks. Actually it's very good to see you."

Another pause.

"You're looking very delectable," he said. "But then you always do."

Jane thought that at least the trouble she

had taken to make herself look her best hadn't been wasted. She had washed her hair the previous evening and gone to bed in rollers, something she hated doing. But she now decided it had been worth it. She was wearing a new dress that she had intended to keep for special occasions and had decided that, if she was lucky, this might be one of them. She racked her brains for the right thing to say. Piers was in a prickly mood, she could see. But it was something that he had turned up at all.

"How's Lawson's?" he asked.

"Same as usual."

"Have they found someone to take my place? Some dedicated, hard-working chap willing to say, Yes sir, no sir, three bags full sir, to old Lawson?"

"They've got someone, yes."

"I wish him luck."

"And you?"

"I told you when you phoned me yesterday, I'm idling my time away." Piers met her eyes. "You, I take it, are a busy little bee as always? Working like a black at the office and at home, writing every moment of your spare time?"

"I'm writing — yes."

"You'll bring something off one day."

"I hope so. Actually I've found work outside the office almost impossible. Somehow I haven't been able to settle to it."

"Too bad. I thought you could always put pen to paper."

"Oh no. At least I haven't been able to for the last week or two."

Piers thought he knew the reason but he didn't propose to ask her. He wondered if Jane really believed herself in love with him. Theirs had been a strange relationship. There had been times when he had believed himself in love with her. At least she had been the only girl who had seriously attracted him. He supposed, despite his twenty years, he was young for his age. He was a little scared of girls. He had never run after them in the way his friends ran after them. Maybe he missed a lot. But when he had considered it he had told himself that there was plenty of time.

He wondered if he should ask her why she was finding work outside the office difficult. But if he did and it was the reason he suspected, she wouldn't tell him.

Jane was wondering what she would answer if he were to ask her. If she told him the truth it would only embarrass him. Could he really be so blind that he didn't realise the way she felt about him? Theirs was an odd relationship. Beyond holding her hand at a cinema and kissing her when the opportunity presented itself, that had been as far as their romance had gone. She supposed they were both young for their age. Certainly she had never had a succession of boy-friends such as her girl-friends had had. But then she had always been shy of boys.

"You'll get going again," said Piers.

"I hope so. It's so frustrating looking at a blank sheet of paper."

"Don't I know it!"

"So you have been trying?"

"Not very enthusiastically."

Jane met his eyes. "I wish you hadn't left Lawson's, Piers. That wasn't very sensible of you."

Piers's face clouded. "Could we talk of something else?"

"I'm sorry. But I do."

The waitress put his plate before him. Piers looked at it balefully. "I thought you said the fish was good, Jane?"

"It is."

"This looks singularly unappetising." He called the waitress back and said it wasn't hot and the plate was dirty.

The waitress glared at him. "This isn't the Ritz."

"I know, but that's no excuse for the plates not being clean."

The girl went off in a huff. Jane sighed. She hated Piers in this mood. She could see he was out to pick a quarrel with anybody. She only hoped she wouldn't be the next victim. But it would be a miracle if she escaped.

By the time the sweet arrived the worst had happened. Piers said that plate, too, was dirty and lost his temper. So did the waitress. When she had gone Jane lost hers.

"Why I suggested we met I can't imagine. I should have had more sense. You don't know how to behave like a civilised human being."

Piers's eyes were stormy, his face white with rage. "At least it was you who suggested this meeting. I only regret now that I came. I certainly wouldn't have done if you hadn't phoned me."

Jane knew he had gained a point there and hated him for it. But she found it was comforting to be able to hate him. Far more so indeed than being so ridiculously in love with him. She only hoped she could sustain this state of indignation.

"I wish I hadn't phoned you. I should have had more sense. I certainly won't again."

Piers hoped she meant it. He should have known better than to fall in with her suggestion. He hadn't wanted to. Or had he? Honesty made him admit that, until he had arrived and sat down to lunch with Jane, he had been looking forward to seeing her. Now he couldn't think why. She was smug and exasperating and this was the last time he would meet her.

He picked up the bill the waitress slammed down on the table. Jane put out her hand to grab it. Hitherto she had insisted they went fifty-fifty. She had always been adamantly independent.

"I wanted this to be mine today," she said, her anger now abating.

Piers felt even more incensed. "The little wage-earner paying for the stony broke."

"Don't be absurd."

"Well, you aren't going to." He put

down a pound note, left the waitress a far larger tip than she deserved, which he considered magnanimous of him but he wasn't going to have Jane imagining he couldn't afford to stand her a lunch, and followed her out of the restaurant.

Once outside both wished their meeting wasn't ending so disastrously. Piers was thinking that if only they were parting amicably he could have suggested they might meet again when she left Lawson's at the end of the day. There were a number of pleasant things they could do that would cost very little money. They could take a steamer to Richmond or Kew as they had done often before. Or they could go to Hyde Park and take a boat on the Serpentine.

Jane also was wishing they hadn't quarrelled. She too was thinking how much she would like to meet Piers again when she left Lawson's at the end of the day.

But they seemed to have reached an *impasse*. It would look as if this really was the parting of the ways.

"You coming my way?" she asked and instantly wished she hadn't suggested it.

"No, I want to go to Piccadilly."

"In that case it's good-bye."

"It would seem like it."

"Well, good luck and thank you for my lunch."

She turned on her heel and left him. Piers watched her trim little figure disappear from sight. He thought unhappily that this really was the end between them. He supposed he had behaved churlishly. But she had got him on the raw as she had done so often in the past.

Too late he regretted that their lunch had been such an abysmal failure. He wondered if by any chance she did too. He doubted it. It was clear that she no longer had any time for him.

6

CATHERINE sat at her dressing-table and looked at herself in the mirror with dispassionate interest. She supposed that, considering this was her forty-fifth birthday, she could easily be looking a good deal older. She certainly felt it. All the same she only needed a tint very occasionally to hide her white hairs and she had few wrinkles. She heard a light tap on her door and Sarah came into the room.

"Will I do David credit?"

"You certainly will."

Sarah had a new dress. It was a soft shade of green that emphasised the green in her eyes. It was simply cut and she had been steered by Catherine from choosing one that was far more elaborate.

She preened herself before her mother's long mirror appreciating what she saw. She decided it had been wiser to choose this particular dress instead of the one she had wanted. That had doubtless been too old for her. She wondered if Garry would like it. She would wear it tomorrow night when they met.

"I thought I'd better do David credit too," she said to her mother, "since this is your birthday party. What time is he calling for us?"

"Around half-past seven. I couldn't make it earlier. I've had a busy day."

"Poor Mummy, you do have to work hard, don't you? But still you won't much longer."

Catherine knew this was true. But she was glad she had got David to agree that she wouldn't give up work altogether. She wouldn't really like to be a lady of leisure. She couldn't imagine what she would do with herself. Running a home for David and the children wouldn't take up all her time. Especially as Annie had already agreed that she would be only too glad to work for them.

Annie had been delighted when she had heard the news. Catherine suspected that she had been hoping for a long while that she would remarry. At first they were all moving into David's flat which he said was far too large for him by himself and there would be ample room for them all. But it was to be only a temporary arrangement.

As soon as Catherine and he could find a house they both liked, they would move into it. That day Catherine had given her house to the estate agents to sell. She knew she would feel a pang at leaving it. It had been her home for so long. The children would be sorry too. She hadn't yet told them that plans were gradually now taking shape for her marriage to David.

Looking at Sarah, thinking how pretty she was, she wondered what was happening between her and Garry Gold. David's advice had been that she should tread warily. There had been no further phone calls from Mrs. Gold and, though Sarah had been out often in the evenings, she had never come home worryingly late. Not, thought her mother, that she intended to let the subject drop. She was merely allowing a little time to pass before she made any further move. She had practically decided that, when she did, it would be to see Garry Gold, if she could find out how to contact him, and ask him point-blank to stop seeing Sarah.

"I say, Mummy, you really do look super tonight. I don't wonder David's crazy about you."

"Thank you, darling."

"Have you used my birthday present yet?"

"I would have done today but I haven't had time."

Sarah's present had been touchingly practical. A facial at Amanda Bruton's where she worked.

"If I were you," said Sarah, "I'd settle for a course. In fact, once you start you need to keep them up. I told David that was what I was giving you and he thought it was a very good idea."

"Did he indeed!"

"He said it very nicely."

"I'm quite sure he did."

"When you go, Mummy, be sure they give particular attention to your neck or I'll have a word with Maureen about it — she's the tops there. I'm not allowed to do facials yet, of course. I haven't been training long enough. I do mostly manicures."

Catherine leaned forward and looked more closely at her neck in her mirror. She couldn't see anything wrong with it. Or was it perhaps beginning to look a little scraggy?

Sarah was blissfully unaware that she was on delicate ground. As the door bell rang she sped from the room, saying she would let David in.

Catherine followed her more slowly. David and she had already lunched together today. Calling to Linda and Piers to join them, she went downstairs to the sitting-room to find David, who was as much at home now in her home as he was in his own, waiting to open a bottle of champagne.

"Champagne cocktails before we start," he said.

"Lovely," said Sarah. "My favourite drink."

Catherine wondered how often she had had them. Never before to her knowledge. But then there was a lot about Sarah she didn't know. It was a disquieting thought.

Linda slipped unobtrusively into the room, wearing a black chiffon dress Catherine hadn't seen before. She looked lovelier than ever, but deplorably thin. Catherine slid an arm through hers and drew her towards her.

"We're only waiting for Piers now," she said.

"I'll call him," said Sarah and went out into the hall and yelled up the stairs: "Hurry up, Piers, we're waiting."

He came a few moments later. Catherine was relieved to see him. She had been afraid that at the last moment he might jib at this family party. She knew it was only out of affection for her that he was joining them. She hoped that the evening would be a success. She had been delighted when David had suggested it. But she had been apprehensive too. Her two elder children were far from easy. She wasn't happy either about Sarah since that fateful phone call from Mrs. Gold.

David opened the champagne bottle. Catherine knew he was equally anxious that the evening should be a success, that they both knew this was a test case because in the future there should be many occasions when they would go out together in a family party.

David raised his glass. "To you, Catherine."

"Thank you, darling."

Her three children raised their glasses too.

"To you," they said in chorus.

David had booked a table at the Dorchester. As they studied the menu trying to decide what they would have, Catherine's mind went back to former birthdays. Always the children set great store by them. They had been red-letter days that she had sometimes thought her family enjoyed even more than she did. She remembered an earlier one, her thirty-third. It had been on a Sunday, so they had all been at home and the children had banished Annie from the kitchen and made everything for the birthday tea themselves. It had been a wonderful one with thinly cut sandwiches and scones and an iced birthday cake with thirty-three candles. Catherine remembered that she could have done without the candles and wondering how they had succeeded in getting them on the cake.

She wished she could put the clock back and that her family were still children. In those days they hadn't given her the concern they were giving her today. Though she had had the sole responsibility of them and there had been the nagging fear that she might fall ill and be unable to support and educate them, there had been less anxiety about them.

It was unfortunate that each one of them presented such a problem at the time when she wanted to remarry. A few weeks ago there would have been no hesitation in her mind about marrying David as soon as he wanted. Linda, as far as she knew, was happy in her job in America; Piers, always perhaps something of an unknown quantity, had seemed to be settling down at Lawson's and Sarah had just started at Amanda Bruton's and loved it.

There was more champagne now. Only as dinner progressed was Catherine conscious that her two elder children were making an effort to pretend they were enjoying themselves. She knew them so well. Linda had a heart-breaking lightness of manner. Piers seemed to be eating scarcely anything. Only Sarah was apparently thoroughly enjoying herself.

"It's been a lovely party," she said as they drove home. "Thank you, David. I'm awfully glad you're going to marry Mummy By the way, have you decided when yet?"

Catherine and he had been discussing it at lunch. There would be a lot to be arranged but she had thought it would be all plain sailing. Now she wasn't so sure.

"Next month, I hope."

"Gosh, that's soon," said Sarah.

David smiled. "I don't see why we should wait."

Next month, thought Sarah, would suit her beautifully. Her mother would be bound to go away with David for a honeymoon. Garry was due for a holiday, he had told her, and though she hadn't yet mentioned it to her mother, so was she. In which case Garry and she might slip off together for a few days to Devon. They would go by car and it would all be idyllic and it would also be perfectly respectable.

Sarah had wondered once or twice when she had been considering it whether Garry would be bitterly disappointed when he found she didn't propose to pop into bed with him. Many girls, especially those who were engaged, slept with their boy-friends as far as she could make out, though she had wondered sometimes if they were only boasting. But this was a permissive age. Very different from the one their parents had been brought up in.

Linda too thought "next month" and decided she had better start looking for somewhere to live. She wondered what her mother proposed to do with their present home? Sell it or let it furnished? She sat there in the darkness of the car wondering, with little interest, what life held in store for her. Not Dirk Marion, anyway. Three times he had called at the house since they had met: once when her mother had asked him for drinks on that Wednesday evening, then he had dropped in uninvited a few days later with the excuse that he had happened to be passing and he had called again last evening. Luckily she had managed to avoid him. But he was infuriatingly persistent. She couldn't think why. She supposed she should feel flattered. Her mother had said only that morning at breakfast that Dirk Marion had been disappointed last evening to find he had missed her.

Eventually perhaps he would realise she didn't want to see him. If he really knew who she was and had any sensitivity at all, which seemed unlikely, he would know the reason.

She was aware unhappily that the evening had fallen a little flat. Sarah had been her usual light-hearted self but Piers and she had rather let the side down. The trouble was neither of them was any good at pretending. She knew Piers liked these so-called family outings no more than she. To her they would never be real family outings because David Cullis would never be one of her family.

"Will you come in for a drink, David?" Catherine asked as the car pulled up outside the house.

"I don't think so, darling. It's fairly late and I have a long day tomorrow. So, I am sure, have you."

Catherine knew that neither his long day nor hers had anything to do with his not stopping. He was leaving her tonight with her children. And now they were thanking him politely for a lovely evening, Sarah, with no restraint, her arms round his neck, giving him a bearlike hug.

"It's been super, David, thank you so much for taking us."

"Good-night and thank you," said Linda. "I'll be along punctually in the morning."

"Good-night. Thanks awfully," said Piers.

They went into the house, leaving Catherine alone with David.

"Those three children of yours would, I suppose, be horrified if they knew how much I want to kiss you."

Catherine smiled. "They would be even more horrified if they knew how much I want you to."

He held her close, kissed her warmly, then released her. She watched him drive off in the car, waved, and then went into the house.

Sarah with a quick good-night kiss said she was off to bed. Linda and Piers were in the sitting-room, both looking a trifle odd.

"Would either of you like another drink?" she asked. "It had better be brandy after that champagne."

"A very small one," said Linda, "with a lot of soda."

Piers said he wanted nothing.

Catherine poured a weak one for herself and Linda. Young though he was, she wished Piers would have had one too. She noticed he had scarcely had anything all the evening. And this was, after all, her birthday.

"Well, it's been a very pleasant evening," she said, feeling sure that neither Linda nor Piers agreed with her.

"It was awfully nice of Mr. Cullis to take us," said Linda.

"Linda darling, couldn't you call him David? I wish you would."

Linda smiled. "I'm sorry, Mother. I just can't get used to it. I call him Mr. Cullis, you see, when I'm working for him."

"Still, since before very long you'll be living in his house — "

"That's what I want to talk to you about," said Linda.

"Me, too," said Piers. He looked at his mother anxiously. "I hope this isn't terribly bad timing, I know it's your birthday but neither Linda nor I can let you go on thinking we are coming to live with you when you marry. We didn't realise till this evening that it would be so soon. Now we know it is to be next month, we feel we had better lose no time in telling you."

Catherine sat down heavily in her chair. She wondered why she had been so stupid as not to realise that something like this might happen. She looked from Linda to Piers, all the joy of the evening leaving her, aware of a feeling of bleak dismay.

"What do you propose to do?" she asked.

"I thought I'd like to find a small inexpensive flat," said Linda.

"And live alone?"

"Yes, Mother."

"And you, Piers?"

"I'll try to find some cheap digs. I'll be all right."

Catherine sipped her brandy. She had heard that before. First from Linda, now from Piers. She felt stricken. Now what was she going to do? How could she let Linda go off and live by herself in the state she was in at the moment? How could she let Piers either? Though they would probably deny it, they both needed her. Had things been different, it would have been perfectly all right and quite understandable. Indeed it might have been a better arrangement. Linda was old enough to live on her own. She had had an apartment by herself in New York. But look at the result!

And how could she let Piers go off and, as he put it, find cheap digs? Before he had left Lawson's this would have been perfectly feasible. Though he had been only earning a small salary, with help from her he could have managed. But now there was no small salary and her guess was that he had very little money. Neither for that matter these days were there any cheap digs! True he could get a job — no young man of his age should be out of work—but she didn't want him to be forced to take one he wouldn't like.

No, everything had changed since she had said she would marry David.

"I'm sorry, Mother, I hope you don't mind our not wanting to live with you," said Linda.

"I would much prefer you did."

Linda and Piers exchanged glances.

Piers said: "I know, but we are both sure it just wouldn't work. Anyway, we don't think it fair to David."

"Isn't he the best judge of that?"

"Mother, please don't be difficult about this," said Linda. "Even though we won't be living with you, you'll see plenty of us."

Catherine wondered if this would be true. She could see them drifting away from her. Even this she could bear if she knew they were happy.

"You'll still have Sarah," said Piers.

Catherine sighed. Sarah too, though the other two didn't know it, was also a problem. One that she would have to tackle before long. Certainly before she married David. In fact, the longer she delayed, the more difficult it could become.

"All right, darlings, if you both want to be on your own, I won't try to dissuade you. And, anyway, there is no need for either of you to start making fresh plans at the moment."

"But, Mother, Mr. Cullis — I'm sorry, I mean David — said he hoped you would be married next month." Linda said.

"I know, but it's not definitely fixed yet. There's a great deal to be seen to first. I've got to get things settled about this house. I have clothes to buy. Believe it or not, I'm going off on a honeymoon and though I may be far too old for anything like that to you two, David has very different ideas on the subject."

Linda kissed her mother and said she was adorable, and that she didn't look a day more than thirty. She supposed, as she said this, that possibly her mother didn't look so young as that but she certainly didn't look her real age. That must be because she was so happy, because David and she were so much in love. She caught a glimpse of herself in a mirror and knew that she looked old for her age. But there had been a time — and not long ago — when she, too, had looked far younger. She, too, had had that glow her mother had. It wasn't necessarily a matter of years that made a woman look young. Happiness had far more to do with it.

Piers also thought his mother looked surprisingly young. In fact, he had never seen her look so radiant as she looked this evening. He wished that now that radiance didn't seem to be fading, that she wasn't instead looking worried and anxious. Linda and he were responsible. It was too bad that they had cast a gloom on what had otherwise been such a successful evening.

"I think we should go to bed," said Catherine, feeling suddenly so tired that she didn't want to stay up a moment longer. "Will you lock up and put the lights out, Piers?"

Linda slipped her arm through her mother's as they went upstairs together. She hoped her mother wouldn't delay her marriage to David because of Piers and herself. She knew their suggestion that they would prefer to live on their own was worrying her. But surely her mother wouldn't be so foolish? Piers and she would be all right. And would it matter very much if they weren't?

As he followed them both, switching off the light in the hall as he passed, Piers was thinking along the same lines. He didn't want to continue living at home with nothing to do any longer. In fact the sooner he got a job, any kind of job, the better. The small capital left him by his grandmother a few months ago was rapidly dwindling. He had better stop kidding himself that he could make any money at writing. He supposed he had been a damned fool to leave Lawson's but it was useless to regret that now.

He caught a swift look of unhappiness as he bent to kiss his mother good-night and wondered if Linda and he were behaving very badly. She had done so much for them, worked like a slave since their father died to keep them and educate them. He hoped, when she married David, she would be very happy.

7

LINDA put the cover on her typewriter and went into David's consulting-room to tidy his desk and lock the windows. He had left a few minutes ago. She thought how lucky her mother was to be marrying him. As he was to be marrying her mother. She hoped their marriage wouldn't cut across her own path too ruthlessly, though she supposed this was selfish. But she so dreaded living alone. When she had left America she had longed to be with her family. At any rate for some time. She had been afraid to be by herself.

She had been by herself in New York. In a two-roomed apartment on the twentieth storey. She shuddered, remembering the many times she had looked out of that tall, soulless building on to the narrow street below. Only the thought of her mother, Piers and Sarah had more than once brought her to her senses. But misery had often nearly driven her crazy. Sometimes to such an extent that she had hardly known what she was doing.

She closed her mind to the thoughts that invaded it, knowing they were cowardly. She had to continue to live though she might think she didn't want to. She wasn't alone in this. Countless men and women felt as she did.

She picked up her bag and went out into the street to start her weary trek home.

"Hi, there!"

She turned to see Dirk Marion smiling at her.

She was tempted to pass him with a curt acknowledgment, but that would be unnecessarily discourteous. But he was the last person she wanted to encounter. By now she must have made that clear to him.

He said: "As you never seem to be at home when I call, I thought I'd waylay you as you left your job."

"I can't think why?"

"I would have thought it was clear to you that I want to know more of you."

"And I would have thought it was clear to you that I didn't want to know more of you."

This was rude. But she didn't care.

"Why? What have I done that you

should be so unfriendly? Here am I a stranger in your country and you are downright churlish to me."

Linda coloured, "I'm sorry, but — "

Dirk laid a hand on her arm. "Look, couldn't you stop being so prickly? How about having dinner with me?"

"I can't. I'm expected home."

"You can phone your mother and say you won't be in till later."

"And if I don't want to?"

"OK. Then come and have a drink. I've found a nice little bar just round the corner from here."

His hand was at her elbow now, and against her will she was keeping pace beside him.

"It couldn't be, I suppose," he said, "because you are scared of what I might say to you that you are so determined to avoid me?"

Linda flinched as though he had struck her. He had asked her the one question it was next to impossible to answer. Because it was true. But only because she was so afraid of what he might force her to remember. Her eyes flashed suddenly. Hadn't this man any sensitivity? If, as she was now feeling sure, he knew why she was avoiding him, he must know it was understandable that she wouldn't want to see him.

They had reached the bar now. It seemed she had no alternative but to have a drink with him.

"What would you like?" he asked as the waiter came over to them.

"A sherry, please."

"Here's luck," said Dirk when the waiter set their glasses before them. And as he saw her looking at her watch, "Don't tell me you're in a hurry."

"I am, as it happens."

"I'll drive you home. I have a car just round the corner. I've hired one for the time I'm over here."

"You'll find it more of a liability than an asset in London. The traffic's appalling."

"Maybe but it's preferable to public transport."

"I'll go home by public transport," said Linda. "It's quite quick for me. I take the tube to Waterloo and then a train to Wimbledon. If I'm lucky I can get one that does it in ten minutes."

Dirk said: "Actually I didn't ask you to

have a drink with me to discuss public transport."

"I didn't imagine you did." And since she might as well risk it: "As a point of interest, just why did you ask me?"

"I told you. I want to know more of you."

"Why?"

"You intrigue me. I told you the first time we met and I'm even more sure of it today, I feel certain we have met before. Maybe mine's the sort of face a girl doesn't remember."

"Could be," she said. "But I don't think so."

"All the same I'm sure I've seen you somewhere." He looked at her speculatively. "Did you ever know a chap called Hank Nickson?"

Linda put down her glass unsteadily. She wished she hadn't been such a fool as to allow herself to be inveigled into this bar to have a drink with Dirk. She should have been more strong-minded. She wondered whether to deny having known Hank and then decided it would be wiser not to. Dirk obviously knew that she had.

"Yes."

"At one time he was my closest friend. Then I lost touch with him."

Hank had never mentioned Dirk to her, thought Linda. But then she had known very little about him. All she had known was that she loved him more than she had ever believed she would love any man and nothing else had seemed to her to matter.

"You heard what happened to him, I expect?" said Dirk.

The colour drained from Linda's face. Oh God, she thought, hadn't this man any mercy?

"Yes."

Dirk, watching her closely, wondered how long it would be before she got up and left him. He wondered if he had been foolish to go ahead so quickly. He had intended first to gain her confidence, telling himself that it would be much easier to bring off what he wanted if he could establish a friendly footing between them. But this seemed so incredibly difficult. Without being unduly conceited he had believed he had quite a way with women. He hadn't had such difficulty with one before.

Linda looked at him.

"Mr. Marion, would you please tell me why you are so curious about me?"

Dirk felt an unwilling admiration for her. She certainly wasn't trying to avoid the issue.

"Because I want to know you better."

Linda didn't believe this. She only wished she could.

"I see."

"I wish you'd change your mind about dinner. London's a lonely place for a bachelor on his own. I suppose that's true of all big cities. You must have been lonely when you first arrived in New York."

"I'd never been so lonely in my life." The moment she had said this, Linda wished she hadn't even told him this much about herself.

"I expect once you got to know people you had a lot of fun."

Fun! The fun Hank and she had had when they had been together! How light-hearted they had been, how gay! It had seemed that they hadn't a care in the world. What good companions as well as lovers. Not that they had been lovers in the accepted sense of the word. She supposed she must have been old-fashioned in this.

She knew from the other girls she had become friendly with that most of them went to bed with their boy-friends. They were perfectly frank about it. Especially those who were engaged. It was unwise not to, they said. Better to find out before marriage that their love-making was going to be all they desired than discover it wasn't afterwards.

But she had never thought along these lines. She had been relieved when she had told Hank this that he hadn't forced the issue. Instead, he said they must get married just as soon as it could be arranged. What need was there to wait? They were both so much in love. There was no doubt of this in either of their minds.

"Tell me what interests you?" asked Dirk.

Faced with this direct question Linda could think of nothing. It wouldn't have been true at one time. She had always taken an avid interest in everything. Books. The theatre. The cinema. Music.

"Do you read much?" he asked.

She couldn't remember when last a book had held her interest. She only wished one would. Still she couldn't admit to this.

"Quite a lot."

"Fiction?"

"No, biographies chiefly."

"I prefer them," said Dirk and decided that Linda certainly wasn't at all the sort of girl he had imagined. Or was she putting on an act? He found it difficult to weigh her up which annoyed him because he had always believed he was a good judge of women.

"That chap I was talking about a few moments ago, Hank Nickson, he was a great reader. Highbrow stuff he preferred. By the way, did you by any chance meet Kate, his widow?"

Linda looked Dirk in the eyes which took a great deal of courage. But she didn't want him to think she was afraid to.

"Once."

"She came out of that tragic affair most unjustly. I expect you knew he left a lot of money?"

"No, I didn't know."

Dirk drained his glass, called to the waiter to bring the same again though Linda said she didn't want a second drink and decided she was lying.

"Oh yes, he left a considerable fortune.

But he didn't leave it to Kate. He left it to some other girl. The whole affair stank."

Linda got up from her chair. She had taken as much as she could. She caught sight of her white, drawn face in a mirror and wondered if people would think she was ill. Another moment and someone would come rushing forward with brandy.

"I say, are you all right?" asked Dirk.

"Perfectly. But I'm going. First, though, I would like to make it clear to you that I know nothing about Hank Nickson's financial affairs neither have I the least interest in them. And I would be grateful if you would not attempt to see me again. That is final."

Dirk lingered on after Linda had left him, pondering on their encounter. What sort of a girl was she really? On the face of it, very different from the one he had expected. He had pictured her as hard and brittle, selfish too, out for all she could get. He had known that first time he had met her at the Morrisons' cocktail party that his mental picture of her had been wrong. On the surface anyway. But he had decided that beneath the surface must be the girl he had made up his mind to despise and distrust. It was absurd to think differently.

He sighed. What concerned him most was that apparently he had done no good by seeing her. At first he could hardly believe his good fortune when he had been introduced to her by Mrs. Morrison and found that, on his first day in London, he had met the one girl he had wanted to contact. He had expected it to be difficult. London was such an enormous place. He had told Kate that it was unlikely that he would be able to trace her. It would be like looking for a needle in a bundle of hay.

There had been a phone call from Kate the morning he left New York. By chance she had run into a girl who had worked in the same office as Linda. This girl had told her that Linda's mother was a masseuse, that the family lived in Wimbledon. The girl thought that Linda had most likely returned to England and would probably be with them. In which case it shouldn't be too difficult to track her down.

He wondered if her mother knew what had happened in New York and thought it unlikely. Linda was obviously a girl who was self-contained. Understandably she was probably now trying to forget the whole tragic affair. He wondered, too, if it was true that she hadn't known that Hank Nickson had left her all his money?

8

GARRY and Sarah were finishing dinner. It hadn't been a successful meal. Garry had had a tiring day, work had gone badly, he had had a row with his boss and he knew that, unless he was careful, he would have one with Sarah. Much as he loved her, there were times when he found her exasperating and this was one of them. It occurred to him that there had been several recently.

Sarah said: "I wish you wouldn't be so bad-tempered."

"I'm sorry."

"I hope you won't be bad-tempered when we're married."

"I expect at times I will. You'll just have to put up with it."

"I suppose I will. Actually, I read in a magazine the other day that it means nothing if young married couples fight. In fact, it's not a bad thing. It gives outlet to their feelings. It doesn't really mean they're not in love with each other."

Garry doubted this. And if it were true, he would prefer not to fight. Emma and he fought far too often. More so than ever now. They had had a flaming row before he had left home that morning. She had tried to pin him down as to what time he would be home. When he had told her he thought he might be late, he would probably be kept at the office, she had asked him if he couldn't think of a more original excuse — that one had whiskers on it!

Sarah sighed. "All the same I hope we won't quarrel, Garry. I'll try not to. Promise me you will too." And as this promise wasn't forthcoming, "We'll have to work on our marriage to make it a success. That magazine article said that too."

"You'll be telling me next you wrote up for advice."

Sarah didn't like the edge to Garry's voice. As it happened she had been tempted to. The "Advice to Young Wives" column was the one she always turned to first. It invited letters and said they would be answered promptly and in confidence.

"How soon do you think your divorce will go through, darling?" she wanted to know.

Garry counted ten backwards. He was by no means sure this evening that he wanted a divorce. He supposed he was a heel but it had been Emma in one of her fits of temper who had some weeks back suggested it was the only solution to their matrimonial difficulties. "What's the use of our carrying on like this?" she had stormed at him. "We'd far better call it a day and be done with it." That had been the morning she had found one of Sarah's letters. While he had been in the bath Emma had gone through his pockets which had struck him as a sneaky thing to do. But Emma, when it came to love and marriage, didn't concern herself with the finer points. He wouldn't have stooped to going through her handbag to see what she was up to even though he had a shrewd suspicion that she, too, wasn't as single-minded as she would have him believe.

He couldn't blame her for this. What was sauce for the goose — but he had found he strongly resented the thought of Emma being unfaithful to him. Still, maybe that was going rather far. Probably the most she was indulging in was a near-love-affair such as he was indulging in with

Sarah. That was a charming way of putting it. He wouldn't have thought of it himself but he had overheard two of the junior typists at the office discussing their love-lives and he supposed maybe it covered a multitude of sins.

Honesty forced him to admit that it wasn't his fault that he hadn't been unfaithful to Emma with Sarah. Or was he being unfair to himself? Sarah, for all her would-be sophistication, was such a naïve little thing. Her background was clearly so respectable.

"I wish you would answer my question," said Sarah plaintively.

"Darling, I can't. Divorce takes time."

"I thought it was speeded up now."

"I wouldn't know. I've not been divorced before."

"You'll never be divorced again," said Sarah. "Once we're married we're going to live happily ever after."

Garry thought this would be highly doubtful. And then that was it even more doubtful if they would ever marry. He wished now that he had never put the idea into Sarah's romantic little head. He must have been crazy. If he had any sense he would stop seeing her and quickly. The trouble was he doubted if this would be easy. For one thing he didn't want to. He supposed in his own selfish way he was in love with her and now after ten years of married life with Emma with all its ups and downs he was used to her. As she was, of course, to him. A trial separation might be a good idea if she would agree to it.

"Talking of marriage," he said, "have you had any more trouble with your mother about that phone call from Emma?"

"No, thank goodness. Mother's very understanding really. I suppose now she's getting married again she's more tolerant. I expect it's because she's in love and she knows how I feel. I did tell you, didn't I, that they are getting married next month? That means I'll be able to manage that holiday we're planning."

Garry sighed. He doubted if the holiday was going to be possible. When he had tentatively suggested it, it had been after yet another almighty row with Emma who had said she was sick to death of the cat and dog life they were living and she proposed to go off for a holiday next month with Susy Roberts, her closest woman friend who was also having husband trouble.

"Where was it you suggested we should go?" asked Sarah. And before he could answer: "Not that it matters where we are so long as we're together."

Garry felt for her hand beneath the table and squeezed it. She really was touchingly devoted to him. Though he was sure that if he faded out of her life it wouldn't be long before some other man took his place.

He wondered as they left the restaurant if the balloon would go up if he suggested putting her on a bus instead of taking her back to Wimbledon. He was tired and he had an idea that for once he would like to give Emma a surprise and arrive home earlier than she expected. Though the chances were, if he did, he might find her out. In which case he would only have himself to blame.

But tonight, oddly enough, he didn't feel like a long lingering good-night on the common with Sarah even though he knew that was in her mind.

"We couldn't have a taxi back, I suppose?" suggested Sarah.

"We could not."

"I just thought it might have been rather nice."

Garry wondered whether to tell her that a taxi would be out of the question because he was out of cash, apart from being short of temper.

They waited at the bus stop, a drizzling rain descending on them. The common, Garry thought, was out of the question. Sarah realised this, too, and thought what a disappointing evening it had been. When the bus came, they only just managed to squeeze inside where they had to stand. Garry wished angrily he hadn't fallen in love with a girl who lived as far out as Wimbledon and then wondered if he were really in love with her. A question he had asked himself quite a few times recently.

The trouble was, he couldn't be certain. He only knew that he found her overwhelmingly attractive — he had from the very first moment he had met her — but he also knew that a day would come when that attraction would fade. Her trouble was she was too forthcoming. She hadn't realised yet that there were times when a girl should keep a man guessing.

When they got off the bus it was raining quite heavily. He hurried her along saying that she would probably be soaked by the time she got in. If he could have found a taxi he would have hailed it, but there was no sign of one.

She clung to him as she reached the corner of the road.

"You do love me, Garry?"

"Yes, of course."

"Sometimes I wonder — "

"Darling, don't expect me to cross the t's and dot the i's in the pouring rain."

"Say it just once."

"I love you, Sarah."

"You don't sound as if you mean it."

"Oh, for God's sake — "

Sarah burst into tears.

Garry felt a swine. He drew her into the shelter of a nearby tree and held her close and kissed her.

"We will have that holiday?" she asked as he released her.

"Of course. Now, off you go. It's late. Your mother will wonder what's become of you."

Catherine had been wondering this for the past hour. She was relieved when she heard running footsteps approaching the front door. She hurried quickly to open it. "You're late, Sarah, I've been getting so anxious about you."

"I'm sorry, Mummy, but there was no need for you to be."

Catherine looked at her bedraggled younger daughter and decided this was no time to question her as to where she had been and why hadn't she come home before, but knew that she would have to tackle her about it soon. She must know what the situation was regarding Garry Gold. But she didn't feel equal to it tonight. Tonight she was worrying even more about Linda, who should have been in to dinner but hadn't even telephoned to say she wouldn't be.

"You'd better go straight upstairs and get out of those wet clothes."

"Yes, Mummy, I will."

Sarah fled upstairs, thankful to have got off so lightly though she had an uneasy feeling that a showdown was only postponed.

Catherine went back into the sitting-room. She switched on the television but as soon as the picture showed on the screen she switched it off again. She couldn't concentrate. She was so concerned about Linda. What was keeping her out so late without even phoning to say she wouldn't be in? It was so unlike her. Linda was always so considerate.

At last again she heard running footsteps. Again she was at the front door to greet her daughter.

"Darling, at last, I've been wondering what had become of you."

"I'm sorry, Mummy."

Here, thought Catherine, was another drowned rat. If possible Linda looked more bedraggled than Sarah had looked. She was soaking wet. Her hair hung in damp strands about her pale face.

Catherine took her coat from her.

"I went to a film," said Linda, "and then I've been walking on the Common."

"Darling, in all this rain?"

"I know. It was stupid of me, wasn't it?"

"Very. Have you had anything to eat?"

A faint smile crossed Linda's white face. "Not since lunch."

"Look, go along upstairs and get out of

those wet things and into bed and I'll bring you some hot milk."

Linda went obediently. Catherine went into the kitchen and put on a saucepan of milk. She was rather glad Annie had already gone to bed. Two daughters coming home late like drowned rats was something she preferred to keep from her. She filled two cups of milk thinking that perhaps Sarah might like to have some too. But when she opened Sarah's door the light was out and a sleepy voice in answer to her query murmured; "No, thank you." Sarah apparently was almost asleep already.

Catherine went into Linda's room to find her in bed looking white and drawn and as if she had been crying.

"Here you are, darling. My cure for all evils at bedtime when you were all much younger."

"I know. It's a lovely, soothing drink." Linda sighed. "Do you ever wish you could put the clock back, Mummy?"

"Often."

Catherine saw her three children again in their nursery when they had been young enough to share a large one together. Three little beds against the walls. Even though there had been difficulties and often she had been very lonely after James had died, they had all been very happy. She could hardly bear to remember those days. It came to her with a sudden shock that she had thought scarcely at all of James since she had fallen in love with David and yet she had been very deeply in love with him.

She looked at Linda and suddenly leaned forward to catch the cup of milk that would otherwise have spilt all over the bed as Linda leaned forward to hide her tears. Gently Catherine removed it from her and put it on the bedside table and put an arm round her shaking shoulders. She let her cry, knowing that tears might ease her pain even though they might leave her feeling ill and exhausted.

When at last they ceased Catherine said gently: "Linda darling, wouldn't you like to tell me?"

"I can't, Mummy."

"It breaks my heart to see you so unhappy."

"I'll be all right. This is something I've got to see through by myself. I will in time. Please don't worry."

Don't worry! As if she could help it, thought Catherine. She was so worried she was almost distraught.

"You're sure, my darling, there is nothing I can do?"

"Nothing, Mummy. There is nothing anyone can do."

Catherine bent and kissed her.

Linda's arms reached up and encircled her neck, holding her closely.

"That's not really true, Mummy. You do a great deal. Just having you and home makes all the difference. I daren't think what I would have done if I hadn't had you to come back to."

9

UPSTAIRS in their rooms the next morning the family heard Annie calling that breakfast was ready. Catherine, about to pick up the telephone, decided the call she had intended to make to a patient could wait. She looked at herself in her dressing-table mirror and was appalled at its reflection. Could the night really have put such years on her? It was all very well for her children and David to insist she didn't look her age but that was only when she was at her best, made-up and prepared for the day. This morning it was a very different matter.

In her room across the landing Linda, too, was wishing a bad night didn't have such a distressing effect on her looks. She supposed she must have had some sleep but she didn't feel like it. She had heard the small hours strike. When Annie knocked on her door to tell her time was getting on she supposed she must have fallen asleep eventually but she didn't feel like it.

She opened her bedroom door as Sarah opened hers. It struck her that her younger sister too wasn't looking her best. There were dark shadows beneath her eyes and little colour in her cheeks.

Sarah decided Linda looked even more washed out than usual and wondered, as she had wondered so often since Linda had returned from America, what had happened over there to make her so unhappy. Because though she was obviously trying to make them all believe nothing was wrong she, Sarah, wasn't deceived for a moment. Neither, she was sure, was their mother.

Sarah sighed as she followed Linda downstairs to the dining-room. It must have been an unhappy love affair. Maybe the man had let her down or maybe he had been married.

At the thought of this possibility all her own misery swept over her again. She wished she hadn't seen Garry last night. It would have been far better if they hadn't met.

For it had certainly been one of their least successful evenings. She wished now that she hadn't tried to pin Garry down to getting a divorce and marrying her. What was it he had said? Not to get him in a corner. She had been foolish to be so insistent.

Still, probably all would be well when they met again. They had quarrelled often before. Doubtless they would again. And next time she saw him she would be very sweet and she wouldn't ask him any questions that he might not want to answer. Such as how much did he love her? Funny, she wouldn't have thought he would have minded that. The more times he asked her, the happier she would be. She liked nothing better than to tell him how much she loved him.

She followed Linda into the dining-room and slumped down in her seat at the table.

"You'll have to be quick with your breakfast, Sarah," said Catherine, glancing at the time, "or you'll be late."

"That won't matter. Madame Amanda never gets in till long after ten."

"That's no reason why you shouldn't be on time."

"I should get away in a few moments," said Linda.

Sarah looked at her.

"It won't matter if you're late. You're privileged. You're working for one of the family. Or you soon will be."

"Well, I'm not yet," said Linda sharply.

The door opened and Piers, in a dressing-gown, a rather grubby scarf at his neck, slouched into the room.

He scowled at his mother and sisters and scarcely answered his mother's "Good-morning."

"Did you get out of bed the wrong side, Piers?" asked Sarah.

"Oh, shut up!" He opened the newspaper and disappeared behind it.

Catherine put his plate of bacon and eggs before him. When he paid no heed to it she said gently: "Do eat it before it gets cold, Piers."

Piers wished his mother wouldn't always say this to him if he didn't start eating the moment his food was set before him. As it was, this morning he didn't want anything. He was sorry now that he had come down to breakfast. He hadn't wanted to but he had supposed there would be trouble and anxious questions asked if he didn't.

"Looking for a job?" asked Sarah.

Piers looked at her over the top of the newspaper. "No."

"Well, you should be. Why should Mother and Linda and I work and you slack around all day doing damn all?"

Piers's eyes blazed. "You mind your own bloody business."

"That's nice language for breakfast, I must say. The trouble with you is you're bone idle."

Piers pushed back his chair and left the room banging the door behind him.

Catherine turned on Sarah angrily. "You had no right to speak to Piers like that, Sarah."

Sarah shrugged but she had the grace to look slightly ashamed of herself. "Well, it's true."

"It isn't and, if it were, it has nothing whatever to do with you."

Sarah, too, pushed back her chair. "I'm off," she said.

At the door Catherine called her back. "I think you should apologise to Piers, Sarah."

"Like hell I will."

Sarah, too, slammed the door.

Linda looked at her mother. "Poor

Mother, what an awful family we are. I wonder you put up with us."

Catherine smiled wanly. "You're not awful and I love all three of you dearly but I could have smacked Sarah."

"Maybe we should all have been smacked more often when we were children. Well, I'm off. Despite Sarah's remarks, I don't consider myself entitled to turn up late at my job."

Catherine looked at her anxiously. "Actually I intended coming to your room before you were up this morning to see how you were. I know David wouldn't want you to go unless you feel equal to it."

"I'm all right."

"I wish you weren't so thin. You don't eat enough, darling. You've had next to no breakfast."

"None of us has if it comes to that. Yours is practically untouched. And as for my being thin — how about yourself? How Sarah can ever have been afraid you might be getting a middle-aged spread — "

Catherine smiled. "Well, I certainly don't want to."

Catherine sat on at the breakfast table after Linda had gone. Usually she had early patients but today she hadn't one till ten o'clock and she was a woman who lived locally. What a breakfast it had been! What had happened to her family that so short a while ago had seemed so happy? True she had never been quite sure how Piers was getting on but Sarah hadn't appeared to be any problem and Linda's letters from America had given her no hint that all wasn't well with her.

But now —

Abruptly she left the dining-room and went up to her room to make a phone call that she didn't want Annie to hear as she would if she spoke from the hall. It was one that she had lain awake considering, it seemed to her, most of the night. One that she had become increasingly certain she must make. It was to David and she made it brief.

"Can we meet for lunch, darling?"

"Of course. Our usual little restaurant. One o'clock all right?"

"Yes, I'll be there."

It was a restaurant where they often lunched and dined together. Happy occasions when their skies had seemed blue and their future rosy. But today dark clouds filled those skies and the future looked desolate. Catherine hoped she would have the strength of mind to go through with what she now knew she must tell David. It was going to be hideously difficult. As difficult for her as for him. But she couldn't see that she had any alternative.

She was there at the restaurant just as he, too, reached it. He bent and kissed her and looked at her anxiously. "You all right?"

"Not very."

"I was afraid you weren't. I know you so well. The tone of your voice when you phoned me — "

"Let's go in, David. No, don't let's have drinks in the bar — we'll have them at our table."

He had booked their usual one in a quiet corner. The waiter stood at his elbow waiting while they studied the menu. Not that Catherine needed to study hers. She didn't think she could eat anything.

She laid it aside. "Choose for me, David. Something light. I'm not very hungry."

"In that case neither am I."

He ordered melon and *sole bonne femme*

and a bottle of Chablis, preceded by two dry Martinis.

When the waiter left them he laid a hand over hers. "What is it, darling? There's something terribly wrong I can see."

"I'm afraid there is." And desperately: "Please don't make this difficult for me, David."

On her way to meet him she had turned over different phrases in her mind wondering how she was going to tell him. But she knew she must. Now it seemed to her that she had known this for some days. Only she hadn't wanted to face up to it.

In the end she said quite simply: "I can't marry you, darling. I want you to take this as quite final."

She hated to hurt him and wondered if he realised how much she was hurting herself. But, of course he must. He could have no doubt as to the depth of her love for him.

"It shall be just the way you want it," he said simply.

For one terrifying moment she thought she was going to give way. If he had tried to break her resolve it would have made it so much more difficult for her. But he was putting her before himself. Taking it the way that would be the least painful for her.

"I hate doing this to you, David."

"I know."

"You're not surprised, are you?"

"No. I've been afraid ever since Linda came back from New York that this could happen. It's because of her, isn't it, darling?"

"Not entirely. It's really because of all three of them. I'm worrying also about Piers and Sarah."

"Anything particular happened with either of them?"

"No, except that they're obviously unhappy. And being extremely difficult."

David's hand covered Catherine's. "Poor you. I've often thought you had too many worries because of your children. I so hoped I could have helped you with them."

"I think you could have done. But — " She shook her head. "It just isn't to be."

"Do you know yet what happened to Linda in America?"

"No. I wish I did. She came in very late

last night. She had been to a cinema she said and then she'd been walking on the common in the rain. For the first time since she came home she cried. It broke my heart to see her so distressed. And I felt so hopeless because there just seemed nothing I could say or do."

"It will pass."

"If only she would confide in me. I feel that in some way I must have failed her. If only she would talk to me it might help."

"Don't worry too much. Children often don't confide in their parents. It's no reflection on you."

There was a little pause. Then Catherine said: "You must find someone else, David." She smiled wistfully. "That should be very easy. You're so attractive to women."

"Think so? Dearest, whether you are right or wrong, and I don't think you are right, there is only one woman I want to be attractive to. There'll never be another."

"But there must be. You're too young to live alone for the rest of your life."

"How about you?"

"We're not talking about me. Anyway women are different."

"Nonsense. Some may imagine they are

self-sufficient enough to live on their own but you are not one of them. In a few years' time things may be very different for you. All three of your children may have left you, married and be living in homes of their own."

"You could be right. But even so — "

"When that time comes I'll still be waiting."

"No, David. You've got to forget me and find someone else. Promise me you won't shut yourself off from other women."

"That's not very possible in my profession," he said with a gentle smile.

"Of course it isn't. You should hear the nurses talking about you at the clinic — and the patients."

David let this pass.

"Will you tell the children?" he asked after a moment. "That we're not after all going to be married, I mean."

"I suppose I must, though I won't hurry to do so. But before long they'll know I'm not seeing you. That's inevitable. But I don't want them to think it's because of them we are not going to be married. If they suspected that, each of them would probably insist on going off and living on their own. Linda and Piers would, I'm certain. They would think that would clear the way for you and me."

"But why? I thought it was decided that, when we married, they would live with us."

Catherine felt disconcerted. She didn't want to hurt David still further.

"I know that was what you and I had planned but — well, Linda and Piers have already made up their minds that they would prefer to live on their own."

"I see. I didn't know that."

"Maybe it's understandable. After all they are of an age to want to be independent. If things had been different, that wouldn't have worried me at all. It's because, as I've told you, they are so unhappy, though probably neither of them would admit they need me, that I feel I must break with you, David."

"Why can't we postpone our marriage?"

"Because that wouldn't be fair to you."

"Aren't I the best judge of that?"

"No. I don't think you are."

David sighed. "I know you say this decision of yours must be final but, as I've already said, I don't propose to look on it as such."

It was her turn now to sigh. “Darling, don’t make things more difficult for us both. As I see it, it’s got to be a clean break.”

“All right. You have it your way. But you can’t prevent me just waiting and hoping — ” he paused. Then he said thoughtfully: “You know, the best thing for Linda would be for her to find some eligible young man to fall in love with her and marry her.”

He made a gesture as he realised Catherine was about to speak. “I know what you are going to say. Her heart is broken and it will take a long while to heal. But you can’t have it both ways. You have been insisting that I find someone else. I’m far older than Linda. Even if I wanted to, it wouldn’t be easy. But at her age — ”

“David darling, I’ve thought of that. That’s why I asked that nice young American, Dirk Marion, to come home to meet her. We met him at the Morrisons’ cocktail party. I’m sure I told you. I thought he seemed quite taken with her. In fact, he must be because he’s been out to the house three times but she hasn’t been in.”

"Doesn't she like him?"

"I suppose not. Though I can't imagine why. I found him charming. I agree with you. She's certainly had an unhappy love affair in New York but I have a feeling there is far more to it than that. What, I can't imagine."

Again his hand covered hers. "Try not to worry too much."

Catherine met his eyes. For the past few moments she had ceased to worry about her children. She was thinking that this was the last time David and she would lunch together. She wasn't going to make the mistake of suggesting they remain friends. Neither, she realised, was he. It's not easy to be just friends when you are in love. Probably they would meet occasionally professionally. But today was their last real meeting. She knew she couldn't bear it much longer.

She looked at her watch. "I'll have to go in a minute."

"I'll get the bill."

"If you don't mind, I'd rather I just went."

If she stayed any longer, she knew she would break down and sob.

David seemed to understand this. "All right. If that's what you want. But remember one thing — you know where I am if you ever need me."

"I know." But she wouldn't contact him. He must be left absolutely free. She wondered about Linda working for him. Would it hurt David to see her day after day? But that problem could be resolved later.

"I'd like to thank you for everything," she said. "Especially for today."

"Please don't. There's no need to. Just take care of yourself."

"I'll be all right."

For a moment she heard her children — all three — assuring her they would be all right. Now she was assuring David.

She said a quick unemotional good-bye to him, and picked up her bag and gloves. She went out to the street, round the corner where she had managed to find parking space for her car.

Her patient was only a short distance away. She could cancel her appointment easily if she chose. But she never failed to keep an appointment for any reason connected with herself. There had been times when, because of Piers and Sarah, she had had to make alterations in her daily schedule. The day Linda had returned from America she had cancelled them all. And though it would be easy now to go home to bed, to draw the curtains and feel sorry for herself, what good would it do her? There was no point in running away from her wretchedness. It would only be there awaiting her tomorrow.

She looked up at the sky which was a vivid blue with little white clouds like cotton wool drifting across it. But as she unlocked her car door a heavy cloud hid the sun from view. The cloud overhung it, as indeed it did apparently the lives of her three children and David's life too. But one day surely all would be well again. This utter misery she was feeling now couldn't last for ever. She wouldn't be able to continue living if it did. Or was that foolish thinking? The trouble was she had no alternative. She couldn't quietly and unobtrusively put an end to it all because life had become too much for her. That would be too cowardly. Anyway, she wasn't the suicidal type.

Besides, she wasn't the only woman who

had been forced through circumstances to end a love affair. It was happening all the world over. She asked herself if it would have been less hard to bear if it had been David who had broken with her? No, whichever way it had come about, it would have been no different. Now her only salvation lay in trying to forget the dream that had been so wonderful these past few weeks. Everything between herself and David was over. And one day, if he had any sense, someone else would take her place in his life.

It was against that day she had to brace herself. She would no doubt hear about it casually. A patient would ask her *en passant* if she had heard that that charming surgeon, Mr. Cullis, was going to be married. "He's engaged to a delightful girl. Quite a bit younger than he is but terribly attractive. I ran into them both at a theatre the other evening. They looked radiant."

When this happened, Catherine knew she would have to take the news without flinching. And she would go home and write him a little note of congratulation. She would assure him, as indeed would be true, that she hoped he would be very happy.

She wondered how long it would be before such news reached her. It was unthinkable that David should remain unmarried, living a life of a lonely widower.

And now she dreamed another little dream, a selfish one, no doubt, and one that she told herself could never materialise. But in it years had passed and again she was at a patient's and the patient was saying: "I've often wondered why that delightful surgeon, Mr. Cullis, hasn't re-married. I'm sure he must have been in love with some woman since his wife died. After all, it is many years ago now."

And then there was still one more dream. As David had said would happen with the passage of time, Linda, Piers and Sarah had all married and left her to live their own lives. In her imagination she heard David saying: "Catherine dearest, it's been a long while but I was sure if I waited — "

As she stopped her car outside her patient's she looked up at the sky. The dark cloud had now passed and the sky was a brilliant blue again. Resolutely she rang the bell of her patient's flat.

10

IT was a week later. Catherine and Sarah were alone after dinner. Linda had said she had a headache and had gone to bed early. Piers was out. Sarah wondered if her mother were really interested in the television programme they were watching. She didn't appear to be. It didn't interest her either. Sometimes the telly could be depressingly boring.

"Dull, isn't it, Mummy?"

Catherine had thought the fulsome comedy was one of the worst she had had the misfortune to see. Really some of the programmes were an insult to the viewers!

"Shall we switch it off?" Sarah asked.

"By all means."

Sarah turned the switch and sat back in her chair again. She wondered how she could broach the subject that was uppermost in her mind. It couldn't be left much longer. Her holiday now was only a fortnight away. Garry was taking his at the same time. His wife, he had told Sarah, was going away on a cruise with a woman friend so the coast would be clear for them to go off in his car down to the West Country.

There had been no more talk of his divorce and Sarah had, with great restraint, refrained from making any further reference to it since the last time she had had that dreadful scene on the common. It was a subject that needed to be broached with extreme tact and timing. But when they were away together it shouldn't be too difficult. After all, she didn't doubt for a moment that he was in love with her and wanting to be free to marry her.

"Mummy?"

"What is it, darling?"

"How's David? He's not been here for a week or two. Not since that night he took us all out on your birthday."

"He's very busy just at the moment." Catherine didn't feel equal to telling Sarah the truth. Not just yet. The wound was still too raw.

"All the same, it's a long while."

"Darling, please don't chatter. Now we've got your beloved TV off I'd rather like to get on with my book."

Sarah was silent for a few minutes while

she idly turned the pages of her favourite teenage magazine. Then, bored with it, she put it down.

"Mummy?"

"Yes, darling."

"Can I ask you something?"

"Of course." Catherine felt a certain uneasiness. Sarah was always so outspoken. "What do you want to know?"

"I just wondered when David and you were going to get married? After all, he said on your birthday that it would be in about a month."

"I know, but he didn't realise, as I said to Linda and Piers that night, what a lot had to be seen to first. We've got to find somewhere to live."

"I thought he had a flat of his own large enough for you and any of us you wanted to take along with you?"

"So he has. But talking it over, we decided we would like to start our married life together somewhere new."

Sarah couldn't see the sense in this. It wasn't as if David and her mother were young. The next thing would be her mother saying she wanted to buy a trousseau.

"Also I must get some clothes," said Catherine.

Sarah smiled. How right she had been!

"That shouldn't take you long. The shops are full of the loveliest things. And at least you're stock size." She looked at her mother and smiled. "I hope David appreciates what a lovely figure you have." Then she spoilt it all by adding: "Especially since you are — well, you won't be offended, will you? — but you are middle-aged."

"No, darling, I'm not in the least offended. All the same I don't want to rush things. Neither does David."

Sarah wasn't deceived. She was certain that something had gone wrong between her mother and David. And if that were the case, it would be painful for her mother to talk about it, so she had better leave the subject for the time being. But it was all very tricky. One thing she was determined about: she was going off for her holiday with Garry and nothing was going to prevent her.

Too late Catherine wished she had been frank with Sarah now that the opportunity offered. After all, she couldn't delay indefinitely telling her children that she wasn't going to marry David. But she didn't want to talk about it yet.

And, trying to change the conversation, she walked right into further trouble.

"By the way, Sarah, your holiday is coming very shortly, isn't it?"

"Yes. In a fortnight."

"I was thinking it must be about then. I'm sure David would let Linda have a couple of weeks off and I thought—if we could persuade Piers to come too—we might have a family holiday together."

Sarah looked at her mother aghast. Something must certainly be wrong. If her plans to marry David were going ahead smoothly, she wouldn't suggest anything like this!

Catherine saw the dismay on Sarah's face and her own desperate unhappiness ceased momentarily and gave way to anxiety about Sarah. What had the child in mind for this coming holiday?

"Wouldn't it be nice for us all to have a holiday together?" she suggested. "We've had a lot in the past."

"But, Mummy, won't David hate that?

I mean us all going away and sort of leaving him out in the cold?"

"I'm sure he won't. David is always so occupied he never thinks about holidays."

"But he must be thinking about a honeymoon with you?"

"That's different."

Again Catherine reproached herself for being a coward. And even if they suspected she wasn't marrying David because of them, it could make no difference. But she didn't want to make them feel responsible.

Sarah was now becoming increasingly certain that her mother was hiding something from her. And what that something was: David and she were not, after all, going to marry. But why? The answer was glaringly clear to her. Her mother was imagining she couldn't leave her three children, who, after all, thought Sarah sagely, weren't children any longer. She sighed inwardly. She supposed that was the trouble with parents. They could never believe their children grew up.

"I don't think somehow, Mummy, that's much of an idea," she said.

"Why not, Sarah?"

"Well, Linda and Piers don't seem

exactly in holiday mood. The way those two are at the moment to spend a fortnight away with them would be sheer hell."

Catherine looked at her reproachfully. "Darling, that's a horrid thing to say. I'm sure it wouldn't be."

Sarah shrugged. "I think it would be. Anyway, I only get a fortnight's holiday a year and I want to make the most of it."

Catherine leaned forward in her chair. "Have you anything in mind, darling?"

Sarah hesitated. This wasn't going to be easy. But it had to be said.

"I've arranged to go off with Garry in his car down to the West Country."

Catherine braced herself. She wasn't entirely surprised to hear this. It had been something she had feared but had resolutely closed her mind to.

"It's all going to be perfectly respectable," went on Sarah, "in case you're afraid it won't be. We shall each have our own room. After all, engaged couples often go away for holidays together."

Catherine wondered how best to cope with this situation. She knew she must tread warily.

"Do you consider yourselves an engaged couple, darling?" she asked.

"Of course we do. After all we are going to be married just as soon as Garry's divorce is through."

"Things have gone as far as that, have they? Does this mean that his wife has agreed to one?"

Catherine saw the colour flood Sarah's cheeks at this question and felt quite sure she knew the answer.

"I imagine so."

"You don't know definitely?"

Sarah wished this conversation had never started: she didn't want to lie to her mother.

"Well, Garry talks as if she has."

There was a little pause.

Then Catherine said: "I think, in that case, I should meet him, don't you?"

"Do you want to?"

"Naturally I do if he is likely to become my son-in-law. When are you seeing him again?"

"Tomorrow."

"Then ask him to come here to dinner one evening. Tell him I've suggested it."

Sarah hedged. "The trouble is, he rarely

knows till the last minute if he'll be free on any particular evening. PROs often have to see clients after ordinary office hours."

"Well, at least you can tell him I'm anxious to meet him. He must surely be able to arrange to be free one evening."

Sarah's uneasiness deepened. She had a horrid feeling that Garry wouldn't want to meet her mother. Devoted though she was to her, there were times when Sarah considered her mother far too conventional. And Garry didn't like conventional people. She was quite sure they wouldn't get on together. This was a pity but it couldn't be helped. Perhaps when Garry's divorce was through and they were married things would be different. After all, whether he liked it or not, he would be one of the family. But at the moment he was wont to say that he didn't like ordinary people who lived ordinary lives. He classed them as morons. All his friends were artistic and interesting people who were authors or artists and were picturesque and exciting.

Garry had wanted to be a writer but, though he had tried to write books and short stories, he had sold nothing, so in order to keep body and soul together he had become a PRO. That had been some few years ago. Now he was apparently quite successful in his profession.

"I'll ask him, of course, Mummy, but you mustn't be offended if he can't make it."

"Well, anyway, I suggest you ask him. After all, if one day you hope to marry him, isn't it natural that I should want to meet him?"

Catherine wondered if she was taking the right line. Was it wise to let Sarah believe that she would agree to her marrying Garry? And then she realised with a little shock that if Sarah were determined to do so and he really did get a divorce she, Sarah's mother, would have no say in the matter. At eighteen Sarah was free to marry whom she liked. And there wasn't long to wait till her eighteenth birthday.

She wished she had David still in her life. He would give her sound advice and help with her children. It seemed to be becoming increasingly difficult to cope with them single-handed.

11

PIERS wandered into Foyle's. Bookshops had always held a fascination for him. He glanced longingly at the closely packed shelves of new novels with their colourful wrappers, many with bands round them. Book Society Choice. *Evening Standard* Book of the Month. Well-known names of well-known authors who made large incomes. If only he were one of them! If only there were a faint hope that one day he might be.

Not that he would particularly want to join the best seller ranks though it would be nice to make a lot of money. But he would be satisfied if he could write books that would bring him in a modest income. Books that didn't appeal to the masses but which were well-reviewed and read by people who were discriminating about their reading.

He moved on into the second-hand department. There were several books here he would like to have been able to buy but he had no money to spare. He was, in fact, running perilously low in funds. The legacy his grandmother had left him was fast disappearing.

There had been several times recently when he had realised that he had behaved stupidly in leaving Lawson's. True, it had been an irksome job: but if he hadn't walked out so impulsively he might eventually have been given one more to his liking. It was that he suddenly felt he couldn't stand it a day longer. He had believed that, given a little time, he would have begun to make money at writing.

He knew now that he had been wrong. Not one single acceptance had he had of the various short stories and articles he had sent out. He supposed it was time he faced the fact that it was useless to persevere any longer. Once funds ran out, he couldn't live on his mother indefinitely. As it was, she was giving him a roof over his head and three meals a day and it was high time he became self-supporting.

And this, anyway, couldn't go on much longer. She would surely soon be going to marry David. He wondered if they had yet fixed a definite date for their wedding.

He wondered, too, why he hadn't seen David recently. Usually he dropped in on them quite frequently. And though he hadn't much liked the idea of his mother remarrying and the home breaking up, he knew that had been selfish. His mother deserved a happier and easier life than she had had since his father had died. It couldn't have been much joy bringing up Linda and Sarah and himself single-handed.

And it would look as if now all three of them were causing her concern. Linda obviously had returned from New York desperately unhappy. She might try to make them believe all was well with her but he wasn't deceived. And Sarah had clearly something on her mind. She had been touchy and difficult these past few weeks. As for himself—he knew his mother worried about him and longed for him to get a settled job again.

"Hi, Piers!"

He turned to find Jane beside him. He had not seen her since their last disastrous lunch together. He wished he hadn't run into her today. He hadn't wanted to see her until he could tell her he was beginning to make his way as an author, which he would remind her was something he had always wanted to be. Now she would be bound to ask him how he was getting along and he wasn't going to enjoy answering her.

"How's life?" she asked.

"Fine," he lied and hoped she would believe him. "How's it with you?"

"All right."

"Still at Lawson's?"

"Yes. But as you know, I've always liked it there."

"Damned if I did."

"What are you doing?"

"Writing."

Jane wondered if she dared ask him if he was selling what he wrote and decided it might be tactless.

"I'll send you a book token for your birthday," she said. "That's what I always like best for mine. I had three on my last. Your birthday's the week after next, isn't it?"

Piers felt flattered that she had remembered. And then guilt that he hadn't remembered hers which surely had been only a week ago? They were both under the same birth sign, Leo, which he had been inclined to think was why they had been attracted to each other.

But they weren't any longer. Or was he still attracted to Jane? She was looking quite ravishing this morning. He hadn't seen her in that get-up before. The deep blue coat with a glimpse of a matching dress beneath accentuated the colour of her eyes.

"Yours was last week, wasn't it?"

"Yes. My twentieth. I'm getting quite an old lady."

"Don't be silly. Damn, I'm sorry I forgot it. I should have remembered it."

"I didn't expect you to. Not after our last meeting."

Piers didn't wish to be reminded of it.

"All the same I wish I had," he said. "I can't think how you remembered mine."

"I keep a birthday book."

"With the names of all your boy-friends in it?"

Jane let this pass.

"You took me out on my last birthday. We took a steamer up the river to Hampton Court. But you've probably forgotten."

Piers hadn't. He remembered it vividly. He had only known her a few weeks. It had been a hot summer's evening and Jane had been wearing a blue dress, the same blue as she was wearing today but it had been of a more summery material because there had been a heat-wave. It had been a mini, too, and Jane had the sort of legs that could wear the shortest of short skirts. He glanced down at them briefly and was glad that she wasn't wearing one of those hideous long maxis such as many girls were wearing today. He remembered what a marvellous time they had had, how well they had got on together, how different she had seemed from the chattering vapid girl-friends Sarah brought home.

Jane sighed.

"It seems a long while ago."

"Just over a year."

"A lot has happened since then."

"It has indeed."

"You've left Lawson's."

"My mother's going to remarry."

"Really? Are you pleased? Do you like your future stepfather?"

"Quite. But it'll be a bit of an upheaval. I'll have to find somewhere to live."

Jane wondered how he would manage. If, as she suspected, he wasn't making any money it could be very tricky. She knew, because he had told her on one occasion, that some while back he had been left a legacy by his grandmother but she had an idea it hadn't been very much. Besides money went nowhere these days. Inflation, which seemed to be rapidly on the increase, was sending prices rocketing. She supposed she was lucky to be the daughter of comfortably-off parents and could live at home, paying, because she had insisted, a quite inadequate sum for her keep.

Piers had met her parents a few times in the days when they had been such good friends and she knew they had liked him. Only a week or so back her mother had asked her what had become of that nice young man who worked at Lawson's and whom she used to bring home occasionally. She had answered that he had left the firm and so she rarely saw him.

And now so unexpectedly she was seeing him again.

She looked at him. A bookshop was no place for intimate conversation. Not one as crowded as Foyle's in the lunch hour.

"There's a sandwich bar handy. I was going to buy myself a couple and have a coffee. How about you?"

Piers hadn't considered what he would have for lunch. He hadn't thought he wanted any. It was a meal he quite often skipped.

"If you've nothing grander in mind," suggested Jane, "why don't we have some together?"

Piers hesitated. He wasn't sure whether it was a good idea or not. He was so afraid they might quarrel again as they had last time they had been together. And he didn't want this to happen. He couldn't bear it. Life was difficult enough at the moment without adding to it with a first-class row with Jane who, he had to admit, he was delighted to see again.

She laid a hand on his arm. "Please, Piers."

"All right. If it's what you'd like."

"I wouldn't have suggested it otherwise."

"So long as we don't fight."

Jane smiled. "We won't. I'm feeling particularly peaceful today. And it's so good to see you again."

"It's good to see you."

They left Foyle's together. Jane said the sandwich bar she had in mind was only just round the corner. They bought sandwiches and coffee and were lucky in finding a little table for two, rather tucked away from the crowd of chattering customers.

They looked at each other speculatively.

"Well?" said Piers after a moment.

"I'm trying to think of a non-controversial subject."

"How about the weather?"

"It's a lovely day. We're having a particularly good summer, aren't we?"

"Marvellous. The best, according to the papers, for several years."

"Let's hope it will last. It will be grand if we have a fine autumn." And then her hand touched his. "Piers, this is so stupid."

Piers agreed. He thought it was ridiculous for them to be making polite conversation as if they were mere acquaintances.

Jane's eyes searched his face. "We should be able to say what we like to each other. After all we're friends."

"Somewhat prickly ones quite often."

"We shouldn't be."

Again Piers agreed. The trouble was they were. He supposed the fault was his. Or force of circumstances. He didn't like being without a job. Not that he had seriously tried for one. But wasn't it time he faced the fact that, to imagine he could make a living by writing, was foolish? He'd sent a lot of stuff out and he had received nothing in return but rejection slips. Not one word of encouragement from any friendly editor. He began to wish now that he hadn't fallen in with Jane's suggestion that they should have sandwiches and coffee together.

"There are so many things I want to say to you," Jane said.

"Fire ahead."

"You won't get angry?"

"I'm making no rash promises."

Jane sighed. "Now you're making me nervous. And at one time I used to think I could say anything I liked to you."

"Wouldn't it be better not to beat about the bush? I told you to fire ahead. But I warn you you do so at your own risk."

Jane could have hit him. Or kissed him! Still she couldn't do either in a crowded sandwich bar. But he really was exasperating. She was beginning to wish now that she hadn't run into him so unexpectedly.

"I wish you would face up to things," she said.

"I do. I know I'll never be a writer. That I'll probably find it darned hard to get a job and, when I do, I won't keep it."

"That's such a defeatist outlook."

"So what?"

"You shouldn't think like that."

Piers shrugged. "We can't all think alike."

"Fair enough. But the way you think will get you nowhere."

"I'm not sure I want to get anywhere."

"Don't be ridiculous. You know you do." Jane knew that it was really a waste of time to attempt to reason with Piers. If she had any sense she wouldn't. In fact, it would probably have been safer to have kept the conversation completely impersonal. But it wasn't possible. The shattering thing was, she now realised, that she had been trying to make herself believe since their last disastrous meeting that she couldn't care less about him, but it hadn't, of course, been true.

"Look," Piers said, "what does it matter

to you the way I think or whether I want to get anywhere or not?"

Jane wondered what he would say if she told him the truth. If she were to say: "It matters because I'm in love with you." Hadn't he the remotest idea of the way she felt about him? Considering how sensitive and perceptive he was it astonished her that he was so blind. But maybe it was just as well. At least it saved her pride.

"It matters a lot," she said.

"Well, there's nothing you can do about it."

"So it seems." She touched his hand. "I wish you hadn't left Lawson's."

"I'm thankful I did. The damned firm bored me stiff. I had the dreariest, dullest job — "

"If you had only been patient you would have been given a better and more interesting one before long."

"But I am not patient. I never have been."

"Nor apparently have you learned self-discipline."

"You know it all, don't you?"

"But it's true. What worries me so much is what are you going to do now?"

"I don't know."

"You don't care either, do you? That's your trouble. You don't care about anything. You've no interest in what's going on around you, in the world as it is today."

"Have you?"

"Yes."

"I can't think why. This world is a damned awful place. Especially this blasted country."

"I think that's a stinking thing to say."

"You would. You, I take it, are all for God save the Queen and the Establishment."

Jane's eyes blazed. She couldn't bear the bitterness in his voice. She couldn't bear, but for a very different reason, the bitterness in his eyes.

"I wish you'd stop being so cynical. The way you feel now you have only brought on yourself. You consider yourself a rebel. But what have you got to rebel about?"

"A hell of a lot."

"Such as — "

"You, for instance. The way you sit there preaching at me just because you are in a nice, safe job and you think I should be too." Piers had never felt so angry with Jane though one part of himself, the true part that he hated to face up to, told him he was being unfair. But he didn't care. She had got him on the raw. And this quarrel which he would have given a lot to avoid was worse than any that preceded it. And there had been a number. But at least this was the last. They wouldn't meet again. If he ran into her as he had today he would pass her by with a brief nod and tell himself he was thankful he had got her out of his system.

He found it hard to believe that he had once believed himself in love with her. Now he hated her. He found it even harder to believe that, at one time, she must have liked and respected him. Now it was clear that she had only contempt for him. Not that he was going to let that worry him.

"I hate to see you making such a mess of your life," she said bitterly.

"So you are making abundantly clear."

"Well, it's what you are doing."

Piers was afraid that all she was saying was true. She had got up from her chair now and so had he. They faced each other, both openly hostile.

"I'm going," she said, "I wish I hadn't

suggested we came here together. I might have known there would be a row."

"This one," said Piers bitterly, "is the row to end all rows."

"So I should hope. I'm only sorry I ran into you."

"You can't be more sorry than I am."

"To think that we once enjoyed being together."

"Astonishing, isn't it!"

Their eyes met. Jane hoped Piers wouldn't notice that hers were full of tears. He wondered if they could be and decided he must be mistaken.

"Good-bye," she said, "and good luck. When you've written a best seller, please send me an autographed copy."

Piers's cheeks flamed. "You're damned sure I never will, aren't you?"

She didn't answer. He watched her turn and walk quickly out of the sandwich bar. He followed and, as he came out into the street, he saw her back disappearing round a corner. He strolled along wondering what the hell to do with himself. The afternoon stretched drearily before him. He felt no inclination to go home and carry on with the short story he had been working on for the last few days. He supposed he could go into a public library and look through the advertisements to see if there were some job going that he might get if he were lucky.

He paused outside a travel agency. There was a large poster in the window.

"AUSTRALIA — THE LAND OF OPPORTUNITY".

He stood there looking at it and wondering if this could be the answer to his problem. If he emigrated he would no longer be dependent on his mother. He could get there for £10. He still had enough left from his grandmother's legacy to keep him going for a few weeks. He would send Jane a brief note saying he was, after all, going to do something with his life. He was taking a decisive step.

And when he wrote a best seller he would certainly send her an autographed copy.

12

LINDA picked up the telephone receiver. "Linda?" said her employer's voice. "I've a patient coming at half-past four this afternoon I particularly want to see. Unfortunately I'm detained, so will you tell Whitlock to show him into my consulting-room and ask him if he would mind waiting?"

Linda went out into the hall to deliver this message to the butler who answered the door to the patients of the various consultants. Then she returned to the little office adjoining David's consulting-room. She glanced down his appointments. For a change he had nobody after the four-thirty patient. It was odd that he hadn't told her the name of the patient who was coming, neither was it in the book. She supposed he must have overlooked mentioning it.

She continued making out the accounts, her mind only half on her work. She glanced at the calendar on her desk. The weeks seemed to be slipping by very quickly without any further mention of her mother's wedding. On her mother's birthday David had said he hoped it would be in about a month. She remembered how Piers and she had said they were sorry but neither of them wanted to make their home with her and David, and would prefer to be on their own. She hoped nothing had gone wrong. Now she came to think of it, David hadn't been out to Wimbledon for quite a while nor had her mother mentioned him.

Linda felt a sharp anxiety coupled with an almost unbearable remorse. Could it possibly be that her mother, because Piers and she had wanted to live on their own, had changed her mind about getting married?

The possibility appalled her. She wanted to leave her desk, rush out of the house to find her mother and ask her if this could possibly have happened, to tell her that, if it had, then something must be done to put things right, to insist that she marry David. She must not consider her or Piers. Suddenly she saw them both as selfish and self-centred. Especially herself. It was no excuse that she had been so utterly distraught with misery since she had come home that she had had no thought of anything or anyone but her own deep unhappiness.

There was a knock on the door and Whitlock opened it.

"Mr. Marion is here, Miss Duke."

Linda rose from her chair. Through the open door she saw Dirk Marion entering the consulting-room. There was no alternative but to go forward to greet him, to treat him as if he were any ordinary patient, to tell him that David had telephoned to say that he was sorry but he had been detained. Would Dirk please wait?

Dirk said: "I've really come to see you, Linda."

She stared at him. She felt the four walls closing in on her. She longed to rush past him and out of the house but she knew it would be undignified and cowardly. All she could do, it would seem, was to say, as she had said last time he had told her he wanted to see her, that she had no wish to see him, and to go back to her own room and close the door firmly upon him.

"You made it clear last time we met that

you had no wish to see me," said Dirk, "but I'm afraid I must insist you do because there are certain things I have to say to you. That was why I asked Mr. Cullis to let me see you here."

Linda was aghast. "You mean he knows it is me you have really come to see?"

"Yes."

She leant her weight heavily on her hands and held on to David's desk. Why had he combined with Dirk Marion to make it easy for him to see her? And why had Dirk Marion dragged David into it?

Dirk saw Linda's ashen face and the haunted unhappiness in her eyes and wondered what he had let himself in for. It could be something unexpected, but he doubted it. Yet there were always two sides to every story. But Kate's had been so convincing. So had the headlines that had blazed in the gutter press. Linda Duke was a husband-snatcher, a gold-digger and the type of woman he, Dirk, had no use for.

"What is it that you have so urgently to say to me?" asked Linda.

"I want you to let Hank's widow have at least some of the money he left you. She is quite destitute. Until his death during the time he was living with you he was making her an allowance. Now that has stopped and she hasn't a cent."

Linda was appalled.

"But I didn't live with Hank."

For a split second Dirk wondered if this could possibly be true. And then assured himself that Linda must be lying.

"You'll be telling me next that you didn't know he had left you half a million dollars?"

Linda's hands shook. Shivers ran through her, shaking her from head to toe. This couldn't be true. Hank couldn't have had all that amount of money. But how would she know? She had really known so little about him. Only that she loved him.

Ever since the tragedy in New York she had been terrified that one day something like this would happen. Someone would cross her path who would force her to remember. And she wanted desperately to forget. Now she was afraid she would give way. There would be tears that she couldn't withhold. They were already perilously near the surface.

"Why couldn't you have left me alone?"

she stormed. "How dare you come here and suggest I lived with Hank or that I would ever touch any of his money? I had no idea he had left it to me. His widow can have it all. I — "

She sank down on the chair at David's desk, her head in her bowed hands. She sobbed so terribly, so heartbrokenly that Dirk could only feel a deep remorse and pity and ask himself if the whole thing had been some ghastly mistake?

Had Kate's facts been wrong in some quite incomprehensible way and was Linda not the sort of girl she had insisted? If so, he for one owed Linda profound apology. He had behaved atrociously towards her, treated her in the way he had believed she had deserved. But then all he had heard about her, felt sure he knew about her, going on all Kate had told him, had been so despicable. To have felt compassion for the girl Kate had described to him would have been out of the question.

The last time he had seen Linda and had tried to draw her out, he had begun to wonder whether Kate could have been wrong about her? Then he had chided himself for being gullible, taken in by a soft voice and a pretty face. But she hadn't necessarily needed to have been hard-voiced and brazen-faced to be the sort of girl he had expected.

And he had forced himself to feel an even more bitter antagonism towards her. He had reminded himself that Kate had had the dirtiest deal that one woman could mete out to another.

He reminded himself of this again now. That that was why he was here this afternoon, so insistent that he must see Linda and talk to her. He was quite determined to get the truth out of this girl who had taken Hank away from Kate.

He wished she would stop sobbing so heartbreakingly. He told himself that he was a swine to be doing this to her. He wished Kate had asked someone else to track her down and get her, if possible, to give up some of Hank's money. Well, that promise he had got from her easily enough. In fact, she had just insisted that she hadn't known Hank had left her his money.

He felt bewildered. What was the truth? Could it possibly be that Linda hadn't known she had inherited Hank's money?

Was it really true — and suddenly this was to him of the most vital importance — that she had never lived with Hank?

"Won't you tell me your side of the story?" he asked gently after a few moments.

She shook her head. She couldn't tell him. She couldn't tell anybody. She hadn't even been able to tell her mother the other night when her mother had come to her room and found her in tears and had so clearly longed to know what was the matter.

But as she raised her head it was suddenly as if she were looking at Hank and not at Dirk. She was back in the States. It wasn't the past: it was the present. And Jane Leyton at whose house in Scarsdale she was spending the weekend was saying: "This is Hank Nickson, Linda. He's also a house-guest till Monday."

Hank smiled at her. "I'm glad I managed to make it. I didn't think I was going to be able to till the last minute," and to Jane: "Why didn't you tell me Linda was coming, I could have driven her down?"

"Actually she came yesterday," said Jane. "But you can drive her back on Monday."

"Of course I will."

"It'll need to be early," said Linda. "I have to be at my job by ten."

"I'll see you're there. I'm in my office sharp at nine-thirty each morning. We work hard here in the States."

"Don't I know it," said Linda. "But that doesn't worry me. I quite like hard work."

Jane shuddered. "Sounds horrible to me. I lie in bed as long as I can in the morning. I've reached the age when I need my beauty sleep."

Her husband who was fixing drinks looked over his shoulder.

"Aren't you lucky that you can! If I didn't keep you in luxury, my girl, you'd have had to have your nose to the grindstone. Not that it isn't a very pretty nose."

Jane blew him a kiss. "I wouldn't have married you, if you hadn't been loaded."

"You hard-boiled American women," scoffed Hank. "You're spoilt — every single one of you."

"I doubt if we're more spoilt than English women. Linda's English, incidentally."

"You don't need to tell me. Her voice

is soft and gentle and I bet she's not brittle and shallow."

Jane threw him a look over her shoulder as she refilled his glass. "Some girl let you down, Hank? You sound sour. Tell him we don't like him that way, Bob."

Her husband said obediently: "We don't like you that way, Hank."

Hank shrugged. "You'll just have to put up with me then. I do feel sour tonight." And then, looking at Linda: "But not as sour as I did."

This easy use of Christian names! Linda was unaccustomed to it. Even though she had been in the States quite a while, it still surprised her. But the Americans were so different from the English. They seemed to have no reserve. Linda had only met Jane and her husband once when they asked her for the weekend. But she was glad they had. She liked Hank Nickson. Even though she had only just met him she liked him very much indeed.

Jane said later when they went upstairs to their rooms to tidy before dinner: "Hank seems very taken with you, Linda. He's quite a charmer, don't you think?"

"He certainly is. But then you people

this side of the Atlantic have so much charm."

"Do you think so?"

"Goodness, yes. One only has to meet you for a short while and one feels one has known you a lifetime."

Jane laughed. "That can't be said of you English. You take a lot of knowing. Hank's married, by the way, but I think his marriage is on the rocks."

"That's sad. Was that why he was so sour downstairs?"

"I expect so. Actually I hardly know him. He's a friend of a friend of Bob's."

"I thought you must know him well."

Jane laughed. "I thought you said a few minutes ago that we are old friends from the moment of meeting."

"I like it. It's cosy."

"But not like England?"

"Well, no. We are probably a little stand-offish, though we don't mean to be."

"I think some of you are hell." Jane looked at Linda. "Forgive me for being so frank."

"Of course. Mind you, we think some of you are too." Then Linda felt a sudden embarrassment. Colour rose in her cheeks.

"Please forgive me. I'm afraid that was rather rude."

"Nonsense! I like people to be honest. After all, you only gave as good as you got. I like you, Linda. So does Bob. Come and see us as often as you can. There will always be a welcome here for you."

Linda went the following weekend and the one after. So did Hank Nickson. Then Jane and Bob went off to California on vacation and Linda thought quite rightly that would probably be the last she would see of them.

But not the last she would see of Hank. Now all they wanted was to be together. Their love affair had been so swift that both found it hard to believe. Neither had known anything like it before. Though they had made mutual friends, they didn't want to go about with other people.

They were utterly happy just the two of them together. Doing all the touristy things such as taking a steamer round Manhattan; the ferry across to Staten Island; going to the top of the Empire State Building; and wandering in Central Park. They found a little restaurant in Greenwich Village where they lunched and dined. They became well known there. They had a special waiter who looked after them, always saving them a table. One night after they had dined together he said, and his eyes were moist: "You are the happiest couple I have ever waited on." Linda's eyes were moist too. But it was a once-in-a-lifetime romance. It could never happen again to either of them. Of this she was sure.

Now they were seeing each other every moment they were free. At lunchtime, in the evenings. They danced together till the small hours. On Sundays they went out of the city, glad to get away from the roar of the traffic and the fumes from the cars.

When Linda awoke it was the telephone that called her and Hank's voice asking her if she had slept well and arranging a lunch date. Last thing at night, even after he had kissed her good-night in her apartment, the bell would ring and there would be his voice saying: "I just wanted to know you were safely in bed and to tell you how much I'm in love with you."

It was crazy, of course. But it was heaven. Linda couldn't remember afterwards just when it was Hank had asked her to marry him. He had been married before, he had been quite frank about that, but he was now divorced. It quite suddenly seemed to be accepted between them that, having met and fallen in love, they must in future spend the rest of their lives together.

It was one night just as he was leaving her apartment that he held her closely and told her that there was something very wrong about their having to say good-night to each other.

"It doesn't make sense, my darling," he said.

"I know." And then: "But we must," said Linda, thinking of her mother and Piers and Sarah though perhaps Piers and Sarah didn't matter so much but her mother, yes.

"It must be the City Hall then?"

"Why not the Little Church Round The Corner?"

"Oh, no."

"But why not?"

"The City Hall is more romantic."

"I don't believe it. Nothing can be more romantic than the Little Church Round The Corner."

"You're wrong. All the best people are

married at the City Hall. They just sneak off on the quiet and tell nobody."

"I find that hard to believe."

So they settled for the City Hall and that nobody else would be there. When it came to it, there seemed to be nobody either of them wanted to invite. Linda had no close friends even though she had been in New York some time. There had been only one, Susan Parker, a girl of her own age with whom she had formed a genuine and — she hoped — quite lasting friendship and with whom, till a few weeks ago, she had shared an apartment. But Susan had married and gone to live in California. True, she had a host of acquaintances but none she knew well enough to want to ask to her wedding.

And it would seem that Hank felt the same way as she did. Indeed, he assured her that he far preferred nobody to be there. "I want it to be just the two of us, Linda darling. We'll call in outsiders for witnesses. That's often done. Nobody shall break in on us on our wedding day. We'll have it entirely to ourselves."

Linda had always believed she would have a very different sort of wedding. As a teenager she had dreamed of it. She would wear white and a long veil of Brussels lace and Sarah would be her bridesmaid and Piers most likely give her away. Her mother would give a reception for her and everyone she loved and who loved her would be there.

But that would have been if she had married at home. Over here in New York it was very different. If she couldn't have her mother, Piers and Sarah, then she would be content without anyone.

She would have Hank. Nobody else mattered.

The days passed. Her excitement grew. Everything was settled. She had resigned from her job, where she had been personal assistant to a managing director of an insurance company, everyone had said goodbye to her and told her how sorry they were to lose her, and Mr. Lincoln, her boss, had given her a thousand dollars to buy herself "a little parting present".

But she doubted if he would remember her for very long. He would find a new PA and she would soon be forgotten.

That was the way things were in the States. They loved you one moment and forgot you the next. Maybe that was the most sensible way to live life. But it wasn't her way.

The days passed. And now Hank was saying: "It's tomorrow, my love. It's all settled. Twelve o'clock at the City Hall."

She smiled. "I still have a hankering for the Little Church Round The Corner."

"Personally I don't mind where we get married so long as we marry! And, anyway, I'll have you know that the City Hall is one of our most magnificent buildings."

"But mercifully not your largest. I realise, Hank, you consider New York the finest city in the world but I find it rather overwhelming."

"You'll get used to it."

Hank looked at Linda. "This time tomorrow — " he whispered.

She could hardly believe it. It seemed too good to be true. From tomorrow Hank and she were going to live the rest of their lives together. She had no doubt of that. She could only think how lucky she was. All she hoped was that he thought how lucky he was too.

"I should have cabled my mother," she said, feeling suddenly remorseful that she hadn't. "She'll be terribly upset when she knows I have married without telling her."

"Cable her tomorrow."

"I will. To think that she doesn't even know I've found a husband! Come to that, nobody at the office knows that I'm being married. I just said I was leaving. Why didn't I tell them the reason, I wonder?"

"I can't think."

"I can. It's because I've no real friends over here and you are too precious to talk about."

"Actually, I've told no one about you. You also are too precious to talk about. Thank heaven you didn't want a white wedding and a lot of bridesmaids!"

"I would have done if we had been getting married at home. But as I am over here I prefer it this way. Just sneaking off together."

"I've booked a suite for tomorrow night at the St. Regis. Then I thought we would go off in the car the next day down to Miami. I've heard of an apartment, by the way, that I think might suit us when we return. It's overlooking Central Park."

"High up so that I can see the sky?"

"Yes, darling. On the eighteenth floor."

"It sounds very grand and very pleasant. I hope it won't cost you a tremendous lot of money."

Hank said nonchalantly that it wasn't exactly a gift but it was well within his means.

It struck her that she was marrying a man about whom she knew very little. She knew he was a director of several companies and he always seemed to have plenty of money. She supposed she should have questioned him on practical details but somehow she hadn't cared to.

She looked at her watch. "As I'm getting married tomorrow, I think I should have a reasonably early night. I want to look my best."

"You'd look marvellous if you stayed up till the small hours."

"Don't you believe it. I need my beauty sleep."

His car was nearby. He drove her to her apartment but she insisted he left her when they reached it.

"No lingering good-night tonight," she said with a smile. "We'll save it up."

He touched her cheek in a little caressing gesture. "As you wish. I'll call for you at a quarter to twelve tomorrow morning."

"I'll be waiting."

"I'll probably be early. Why didn't I make it eleven?"

"I can't imagine. Or even nine." She caught hold of his hand again as reluctantly he let her go. "Hank darling, we're going to be terribly happy. I just feel sure of it. I hope you do, too?"

"I do indeed."

"It's marvellous to feel so certain."

"It sure is."

"It gives me such a nice, safe feeling."

"Me too." He held her close again and kissed her then reluctantly he let her go. She waved as she watched him drive away.

Joe, the doorman, who had been watching them, thought how happy little Miss Duke looked as she entered the apartment block. She was one of his favourite tenants. A chap kissing a girl good-night was nothng new to him but Miss Duke was a very special girl. He thought how lucky Mr. Nickson was to have a girl like that obviously so much in love with him.

Joe took a great interest in the tenants of the apartment block. Usually Mr. Nickson went up with Miss Duke for a little while. He wondered why he hadn't tonight.

It certainly hadn't been because there was anything wrong between them. He had never seen Miss Duke so starry-eyed.

"Been having fun?" he asked.

Linda was slightly taken aback. Though she had now been in this apartment for several months, she still hadn't quite got used to Joe's familiarity. Or all the others of that ilk, if it came to it. Her hairdresser always greeted her as if they were lifelong friends. So did the milkman. The postman too. There was no class distinction in the States she had learned. A taxi driver would be as matey as a boy-friend.

"You sure keep late hours," said Joe.

"Not as late as usual."

He swung the elevator gate to and pressed the button of her floor.

"By the way, I'm going away tomorrow," she said.

"For a vacation?"

"Yes. For a fortnight or so."

"Some folks are lucky. Where you going?"

"To Miami but not till the day after tomorrow." And suddenly she wanted to tell somebody. "I'm getting married in the morning."

A broad grin spread over Joe's dusky face. "Well, now isn't that just something! Gee, I hope you'll be very happy."

"I will be I'm certain."

Joe hoped she was right. He hadn't exactly taken to Mr. Nickson, but of course he didn't know him and he could be wrong. But in his job he had learned to be a fairly shrewd judge of people.

"I thought that the day I got married," he said.

"Weren't you?"

Joe shook his grey head sadly. "I was for a few months. Then my wife ran off with my best pal and that was the last I saw of her."

Linda's heart went out to him. She was feeling so divinely happy herself and so certain all was going to be well that she couldn't bear to think of Joe's disillusion.

"That was terrible," she said sympathetically.

"I thought so when it happened but she left my pal a year later. He and I became friends again and we both decided we were well shot of her."

"So long as you both agreed on that maybe you were. But I think you were unlucky."

Joe smiled, a smile that was slightly humorous and slightly pitying. "Still you're sure you'll get along fine with your boy-friend?"

"I am indeed. I wouldn't be going to marry him otherwise."

The elevator had reached her floor now. She said good-night to Joe and went into her apartment. She closed her front door and stood looking around her. This time tomorrow — she supposed it would have been sensible to have arranged to leave the apartment for good the next day but that would have been rather a rush. As things were, she was simply going off with a couple of suit-cases full of clothes suitable for her honeymoon. When she returned to New York, she would pack the remainder of her belongings and relinquish the apartment.

She yawned, stretching her arms above her head, thinking how tired she felt but how unlikely it was that she would get much sleep. She was too excited, too thrilled at the thought of her marriage to

Hank in the morning. To think it was to be her wedding-day! A day that she had always dreamed of ever since she had reached adolescence. She had had boy-friends of course. Occasionally she had thought herself in love. But at the back of her mind she had always known she was mistaken, that somewhere the real love of her life was waiting and someday she would meet him. And when she did she would know instantly that he was the one.

And this had happened. She remembered her first meeting with Hank when she had gone to spend the weekend with Jane and Bob Leyton. The impact he had made on her. She remembered Jane saying that Hank had seemed very taken with her.

That had been the beginning. They hadn't looked back. Their love, it seemed to her, had no flaws.

She went into her bedroom, undressed, put on a house-coat and sat before her dressing-table cleaning her face of any trace of make-up. This time tomorrow — her heartbeats quickened. She thought of Joe and wished he hadn't chosen this particular night to tell her that his marriage had ended in disaster. She only wanted to think of happy marriages tonight. Happy marriages such as hers and Hank's was going to be.

But both of them would have to work on it. Doubtless all girls on the eve of their weddings believed all was going to be well but so many marriages broke up, some after a distressingly short time. That could be because neither husband nor wife tried hard to get along together. There had to be give and take on both sides. More possibly on the wife's than on the husband's.

She would give all along the line. She would try to be understanding if things went wrong, to avoid stupid needless quarrels. True Hank and she had known each other only a few weeks but to date they hadn't had so much as more than the most trivial arguments. They had always been so in tune, one the complement of the other.

She must do her best to see that it was always like this. She hoped Hank would too. She felt sure that he was as anxious to make their marriage a success as she was. Perhaps even more anxious since his first had failed.

She wondered why it had failed. He hadn't mentioned the wife from whom he was divorced and she had hesitated to question him, guessing that the subject must be a painful one.

What she must guard against would be their becoming used to each other. She must never take Hank for granted. They must trust each other and respect each other and, above all, must always love each other the way they loved each other now.

She got into bed. The book she was reading was on the table at her side but, though usually she read a little before she put her light out, she didn't tonight. Her mind was too full of Hank and their love for each other. She knew no book would hold interest for her.

A few moments later the telephone bell rang. She reached out her hand for the receiver.

It was Hank as she had known it would be.

"I only wanted to say good-night, darling."

She smiled in the darkness. "You've already done so."

"I know. But I just wanted to hear your

voice again. This is the last time I'll have to phone you to say good-night. Are you glad?"

"Of course."

"It's going to be wonderful being married to you, Linda."

"It's going to be wonderful being married to you. But I've been thinking — we've got to be awfully careful to make sure it lasts."

"It's going to. I've no doubts," and, anxiety in his voice: "My love, don't tell me you have."

"I haven't. All the same all marriages aren't made in heaven."

"Don't I know it!"

"I want ours to be."

"It won't be my fault if it isn't."

"Or mine."

"Good-night, Linda darling."

"Good-night, Hank." She looked at the little clock on her bedside table. "It's just after midnight."

"Our wedding-day already. Now I must let you go to sleep. I'll be round for you in the morning."

They were married at twelve o'clock the next day. The couple who were to be married after them were their witnesses. Complete strangers who were quite clearly sure they, too, were going to be blissfully happy. Linda wore an off-white, simply cut dress with a matching coat and the diamond brooch Hank had given her. She came out of the City Hall and her heart was almost painfully full of utter happiness.

It was a day of brilliant sunshine and blue skies. For the first time it seemed to her that New York was beautiful. Until today she had disliked the sky-scrapers and the streets, many of them like canyons. She had compared it adversely with the elegance of London. But today even the traffic didn't seem as noisy as usual or the people in such a hurry.

They drove to the St. Regis and with the usual difficulty Hank managed to park the car. They had decided to lunch in the hotel and for purely sentimental reasons to dine that night at their favourite little Greenwich Villlage restaurant, waited on, they hoped, by the waiter who had said they were the happiest couple he had ever seen.

And they would tell him just why they

were so happy. Tell him that tonight they were, if possible, happier than ever. That he wouldn't see them again for a fortnight or so because they were going away on honeymoon but, as soon as they returned, they would dine again at his restaurant. They could picture his beaming face when he heard their news.

They went up to their suite. Linda felt a little thrill as the bell-hop put her suit-case down beside Hank's. She wondered if they looked like a newly-married couple. Not that she cared. She felt like telling the world. And remembered that she hadn't yet told her mother.

When the door closed and they were alone Hank took her in his arms.

"Darling, I still haven't cabled Mother," she said. "I think I should do so at once."

"Wait till after lunch. An hour or two won't make any difference." He gently lifted her chin and bent and kissed her, a long lingering kiss that sent her heart racing.

When at last he released her, she looked up at him, her eyes shining.

"I find it almost impossible to believe we are really married," she said tremulously.

She looked down at her gold wedding-ring. "I'm not dreaming, am I? You did really put this on my finger a short while ago?"

"I did indeed. And from now on you are always going to wear it."

"I'll be buried in it," she said soberly. "Remember that's what I want if I die before you."

He looked at her aghast.

"Sweetheart, don't be so morbid. Anyway I insist on dying before you."

"Now who's being morbid?"

"Shall we lunch up here in our suite or downstairs?" asked Hank.

"I don't mind. I'm not sure I want anything to eat. Everything is so wonderful. I'm so excited."

"Let's lunch downstairs. I want to show you off."

But if many people noticed Linda she noticed no one. She had eyes only for Hank. He had eyes only for her.

"Our first lunch together as husband and wife," Hank said smiling at her.

"Our first of so many."

"Thousands and thousands." And after a few moments, "Eat up, darling."

"I've told you. I'm not hungry."

They drank champagne though Linda assured Hank, as was true, she never drank anything till the evening.

"But this is your wedding-day, Linda." He raised his glass. "To you, my darling."

"To you."

"I think it should be to us," said Hank.

They lingered over their coffee, two people so very much in love. At last they were up in their suite again. It was on the twenty-fifth floor with wide windows leading on to a balcony overlooking the Hudson. They stood looking down on the scene far below them. A steamer was chugging down the river looking like a child's toy.

"Remember the first time we took one of those round Manhattan Island?" asked Hank.

"I do. It was a couple of days after we met."

He put his arm round her shoulders and drew her to him as they stood looking down over the balcony.

"We certainly got away to a flying start," said Hank.

She looked up and saw the expression in his eyes and wished that time could stand still. She felt sure she could never be as happy as she was at this moment, never again could she feel such ecstasy, such a feeling of certainty that, like a fairy princess in a child's story book, she was going to live happily ever after.

"Oh, Hank — "

His hand smoothed her hair.

"Dearest Linda."

"I've so much I want to say to you."

"And I to you."

"I can't find the right words." She laughed softly. "It's not often I'm tongue-tied. I know it's foolish but I just feel no two people can ever have felt as we feel."

"I'm quite certain they haven't. You're so lovely, Linda. You're all I ever dreamed a girl could be."

She closed her eyes. She didn't want to look down on the busy bustling streets beneath her or the gently flowing river. Not even up at the sky. She wanted to listen to Hank's low voice telling her he loved her.

Listening to him she wondered if she could really mean so much to him? Was she as wonderful as he seemed to think? She wasn't, of course. She was quite ordinary. Like millions of other girls. Maybe he was quite ordinary too. Like millions of other men. It was just that they were blinded by their love.

She said as at last he seemed to have run out of words, "Darling, I wonder why you love me so much?"

"I'll tell you. I love the way you look, your broad forehead and high cheekbones. Your wide-apart blue-grey eyes with their long curling lashes. I love the sound of your voice and your delicious sense of humour. You've more sense of fun than any girl I have ever met. You're a wonderful companion. And I love you more deeply. You're the only woman I've ever wanted quite desperately. But you must know that, my darling, without my needing to tell you?"

She did, of course. Just as he must know the same about her.

"How lucky we are, Hank!"

"The two luckiest people in the world."

She gave a shaky little laugh.

"When first I met you at the Leytons I wondered when I went to bed that night if by a miracle you would fall in love with me. It just seemed too much to hope for."

"I wondered the same about you. We certainly bowled each other over. And I'm not susceptible."

"Neither am I." It was true with her but it couldn't after all be quite true with him. He must have been susceptible at least once before. Otherwise he wouldn't have married. She brushed the thought of that other marriage aside. Reminded herself that it had been a failure and had ended in divorce. She leant her head against his shoulder and felt his hand stroking her hair. She put up her own hand and caught his and drew it down and kissed it.

"Darling, tell me again you love me. I just feel I can't hear you say so often enough."

"Linda, my darling, I love you."

"And you always will?" Quite suddenly and inexplicably she was aware of a desperate urge for reassurance.

"I always will, sweetheart."

She heard the sound of a door opening behind them. She felt Hank move abruptly away from her. He went from the balcony into their sitting-room. She followed him automatically.

A woman was there, white faced, stony

eyed. She was standing looking at them.

Hank's face was ashen. He looked hunted, guilty, a man caught out and desperately wondering how he could extricate himself.

But from what? Linda asked herself and waited, terrified.

"I saw you lunching downstairs," the woman said.

"Get out," said Hank.

The woman ignored this.

"I asked at the reception desk for the number of your suite. Mr. and Mrs. Hank Nickson. Very interesting!" Her voice was whipped with sarcasm. She turned to Linda. "I don't suppose you know it but *I* am Mrs. Hank Nickson."

Linda told herself it couldn't be true. It was a ghastly nightmare. She was still back at her apartment in bed but soon she would wake and it would be her wedding-day. And then she knew that it was no nightmare. This must be the woman Hank had married and told her he had divorced. Unless that had been a lie, and it was this woman who was lying. But she didn't think so. The expression on Hank's face made it all too clear.

"I'm Hank's legal wife," the woman said.

Linda put out a hand to the back of a chair for support. She felt sick suddenly and so weak that she was afraid she was going to faint.

"Is it true, Hank?" she asked in a scarcely audible whisper.

He came to her and would have touched her but she flinched away.

"No," he said. "It's a lie. We're divorced."

"We are not," the woman said.

"We very soon will be," said Hank. "The divorce should have been through days ago but at the last moment there was a hitch."

The woman looked at Linda.

"You'll be a fool if you believe that."

Linda longed to but she knew she couldn't.

"I don't."

"Linda darling — I can explain — "

Hank was trying to bar her way now as she rose to her feet and moved unsteadily towards the door.

The woman's voice rose, shrilly. "You'll have hard work explaining me away but I wouldn't put it past you to try. You may feel terrible now," she said turning to Linda and her tone was suddenly almost pitying, "but one day you'll be glad I shattered your little day-dream. You look a nice kind of girl, the kind of girl I was once before I met and married this louse. You — "

Linda didn't wait to hear any more. Somehow she managed to walk out of the suite and reach the elevator.

She grabbed her suit-case went down to the ground floor and out into Central Park. She didn't know where she was going, what she was doing, she didn't care. Yet somehow she lived through the hours that followed. She had money in her bag. She went to Grand Central Station and took a train out to Willchester and walked across the hills. She missed the last one back and sat in the waiting-room till the first came in the morning.

She felt dazed with exhaustion, disillusion and misery. When eventually she reached her apartment Joe looked at her anxiously, clearly wondering sympathetically what had happened.

"Mr. Nickson called three times last evening, Miss Duke."

"Did he?"

"He left a note to be given to you the moment you came in." Joe handed it to her and she took it mechanically.

When she reached her apartment she tore it up without reading it. She glanced at the time. Seven o'clock. This time yesterday — but no, she wouldn't think of yesterday. Unless to be thankful that it was over.

In the street below she heard the milk floats rattling by, the garbage men noisily going their way. She heard Joe drop letters through her letter-box. She picked them up. One or two bills, a brief note from Susan from California saying she was having a marvellous time and why didn't Linda go out and visit her. Married life was wonderful, Linda should try it some time. Susan added a post-script. "I hope to come to New York soon for a few days. I'll look you up."

There was a long letter from her mother. How regularly she wrote! How irregularly she, Linda, wrote. Linda tried to concentrate on all her mother had to tell her. Everything was well at home though her mother was concerned about Piers who had now become unsettled in his job with the publishing company he had joined some little time ago. The trouble was he didn't appear to like going in on the ground floor, he had leanings towards becoming an author himself. "I doubt very much if he would make a success of it, Linda, though I may be wrong. I hope it is only a bad patch he is going through and that he'll stick to his job. After all, if he has any talent, he is in the right job to gain knowledge about the types of books which sell well and if he is really keen to write he could start in his spare time. But Piers, as you know, can be very difficult and doesn't take kindly to advice. It's all very worrying. Sarah has just started at *Amanda's*, the Beauty Salon and seems to like it. She's getting prettier than ever. And now — darling — how are you? We all miss you very much though I perhaps more than the other two. It seems so long since you went to New York. I wish you would come home, even if only for a holiday. . . ."

Linda had planned to go home for a holiday with Hank to introduce him to her family. "Mother, Piers, Sarah, this is my husband. Hank — my mother and my brother and younger sister — " But she wouldn't be doing this. She put her mother's letter on her desk. It would have to be answered. "Mother darling, it was lovely to hear from you and to hear all the news. Don't worry about me. I'm fine but rather rushed or I would have written more often. But the pace of New York is so hectic. There never seems to be a moment."

She heard her door bell ring but she didn't answer it. Her letter-box rattled.

"Linda, this is Hank, I've got to see you."

She went into her bedroom and closed the door. She turned on the radio so that she wouldn't hear his voice. She lay down on her bed, her face to the wall. She told herself however dreadful she was feeling at the moment it would pass. She couldn't possibly remain in this state of misery for ever. No girl could.

She stayed in her apartment and Hank came again and again. There was the ring at the door bell and his voice calling through the letter-box insisting she must let him in. She wondered what the other tenants in the block must think and reflected that perhaps it was just as well that those immediately near her were always out all day.

When the telephone bell rang she didn't answer it, feeling sure it was Hank.

In the evening the realisation that she must have something to eat drove her out. But when she reached a nearby little restaurant and ordered herself some food she had the greatest difficulty in getting it down. She asked the waitress for her check.

"But you've hardly had anything. Didn't you like it?"

"Yes, but I'm not hungry."

When she got back to the apartment Hank was in the foyer. She almost turned and walked swiftly away but Joe was there.

Hank came to her and would have taken her hands but she wouldn't let him.

"I've got to talk to you, Linda. There are things you don't understand."

Linda knew they couldn't have a scene before Joe. Reluctantly she let Hank go up with her to her apartment. When they reached it and the door was closed on them he would have taken her in his arms but she backed away.

"No, Hank."

"Darling, you can't do this to me."

"What have *you* done to *me*?"

"I told you yesterday — I can explain."

"You've no need to."

"But I'm so much in love with you, Linda. I can't live without you."

She wished that in her heart she didn't echo his words. She wished she could kill all feeling for him. Heaven knew it shouldn't be difficult. But now that they were together again she realised she was in danger of relenting. Yes, despite what had happened.

She braced herself. She wasn't going to. She would regret it if she did. It was sheer weakness even to consider it for a moment. If he had told her the truth it might possibly have been different. But to deceive her — to go through a form of marriage with her —

"Kate and I were getting a divorce," Hank said desperately. "It was quite true when I told you that yesterday. I had believed it would have been through by then. But there was a last minute hitch — "

"Such as?"

Hank hesitated a moment. She could feel him struggling with himself to tell the truth. A last desperate effort perhaps to be honest with her.

"She changed her mind. I only knew it three days ago."

"You could have told me then."

"I was afraid to. I thought it might mean I would lose you. Linda darling, won't you come back to me? Live with me as my wife. To me you are my wife."

"No, Hank, I won't do that." But she knew she would probably have agreed if he had been honest with her from the first. After all plenty of girls were living with their boy-friends. It was quite an accepted thing. Her mother would probably be regretful but she would also be understanding. Her mother knew that standards had changed since she had been a young married woman.

"Please, Linda — darling, I beg you to."

"I can't."

His face was white, his eyes distraught.

"I'll shoot myself if you won't."

"Is that blackmail?"

"Call it what you like. I mean it."

She told herself that of course he didn't. And that people who threatened suicide didn't carry it out.

"I can't come back to you," she repeated.

"Because you're no longer in love with me?"

Oh God, she thought, if he would only go! Of course she was in love with him. As much in love with him as she had always been and as she was sure she would always be. But she no longer respected him. And love without respect was worthless.

"Is that it, Linda?" he insisted.

She didn't answer. He stood there looking at her, his eyes beseeching her. She was torn with pity for him for she knew how much he was suffering. But so was she. And it was his fault they were both feeling so terrible.

Then he turned and left her. She heard the door of the apartment close behind him, the elevator coming up to her floor and the gate opening and closing and then the sound of it descending. She went to the window and looked down on him walking along the street, his head bowed, his shoulders slumped. That, she thought, would be the last time she would see him. Unless they ran into each other some-place though she thought it was unlikely. And if they did they would meet as mere acquaintances.

He was out of sight now. She turned away from the window. She looked at the time. It was only a quarter past nine. Somehow the rest of the evening had to be got through and then the night and the day that would follow. And all the days and nights after that. She wondered what she would do. Get a job, she supposed. And as soon as possible. Far better to have something to occupy her mind, her time. She could probably go back to her old one. At the moment she knew her boss had only a temporary PA. He would doubtless be delighted if she went to him and said if he would take her on again she would be pleased. No, after all she wasn't going away. She would be remaining in New York.

But might it not be an idea to go off somewhere new? First-rate Personal Assistants were always in demand. An agency could probably fix her up in Canada or perhaps the West Coast.

It was too soon though to try to make plans. She was too emotionally exhausted. Luckily she had some money saved so there was no need to worry financially.

It was two days later that her door bell rang just as she was waking. She lay listening to it, wondering if it were Hank again. There had been no word from him yesterday for which she was relieved. She supposed he had accepted her decision that she was through with him.

The bell rang again. But it wasn't the insistent ringing that had told her Hank was outside the door. Nor was there any rattling of the letter-box. She reached for her dressing-gown and thrust her feet into slippers and ran a comb through her hair.

Now it rang a third time. She went to the door and opened it. A young man with keen alert eyes looked at her interrogatively.

"Miss Duke?"

"Yes."

"Could you spare me a few moments? I apologise for calling so early."

She frowned.

"I don't know you. Why should you want to see me?"

"I would be grateful if you would."

He gave her no chance to refuse. Already he was inside the door and had closed it behind him. She had no alternative but to precede him into her living-room.

"I just want to ask you one or two questions, Miss Duke."

"What about?"

"You knew Hank Nickson, I believe?"

Knew Hank Nickson. Linda's heart turned to water. She felt the colour drain from her cheeks. She braced herself against whatever might be coming.

"There was a photograph of you on the table beside Mr. Nickson's bed."

She felt icy cold. Suddenly she was terrified.

The young man looked at her more closely.

"I thought perhaps you would have known already. Hank Nickson shot himself in his apartment last evening."

She closed her eyes. Her hands reached out for support to the table in front of her. She mustn't faint. She mustn't faint. She kept repeating this to herself, willing herself not to. But never had she felt so sick and ill. She heard Hank's voice again threatening to shoot himself, her own accusing him of blackmail. And her conviction that people who threatened suicide didn't carry it through. But Hank had. This young man had just told her so. Oh

God, if only she had agreed to go back to him, to live with him as his wife as he had begged her to.

The young man was looking at her anxiously.

"I say, are you all right? Can I get you something?"

She sank down in a chair, her head bowed in her hands. She murmured that she was perfectly all right. It was just that she was so shocked. She had no idea —

"I shouldn't have blurted it out like that."

She raised her head.

"Don't worry. As I've just said — it was such a shock." She hesitated. Then she said, her voice shaking, "Now would you please go?"

"Must I? I don't like to leave you like this. Besides — well, couldn't I ask you one or two questions?"

The penny dropped.

"You're a reporter, aren't you?"

"Yes."

Didn't he realise that he was prying into private grief? Something that the Press wasn't supposed to do.

"There's nothing I can tell you."

The young man looked at her pleadingly. "I don't want to appear unfeeling but I have to do my job. Hank Nickson was in love with you, wasn't he?"

"I've told you — I can't tell you anything."

"I won't ask many questions. I only want the human angle."

She was almost at the end of her tether. She held open the door. "Will you please go?"

But as he obeyed her the elevator stopped at her floor and two other men got out. One was carrying a camera. She slammed the door to and locked it but not, she feared, before he had taken a picture of her. She went to the telephone and rang down to Joe.

"If anyone wants me, Joe, say I'm out."

"Okay, Miss Duke."

But she had overlooked the tradesmen's lift. This could be used by anyone coming in at the back of the block unseen by Joe. A few minutes later another reporter was knocking on the kitchen door that opened out on to the fire-escape. She slammed it in his face and locked it. Then she went back into her living-room and sank down in a chair. Hank was dead. He had carried out his threat to kill himself. She could think only of that. Hank was dead.

She found it hard to believe. Now she was numb with shock. She couldn't take in what had happened. Again she thought it must be some terrible nightmare. This sort of tragedy didn't happen to her. She was a quiet ordinary girl to whom nothing sensational happened. She came from a quiet ordinary family. She felt as if she wasn't Linda Duke any longer but someone quite different. She sat there throughout the morning. Around midday she made herself some coffee. Then she lay down on her bed. She had taken the telephone receiver off the hook. Joe it seemed was guarding her well. There were no further rings at her front-door bell.

She was unaware of the passing hours. Only when at last the light began to fade did she realise that the day was drawing to a close. She got up and went to the dressing-table and looked at her reflection in the mirror. Her eyes were dark and haunted. She looked years older. The way she would look perhaps when she was well into middle-age.

Because Hank was dead. This had brought about the change in her. He had died because she had refused to have anything more to do with him. He had proved that it wasn't true that people who threatened to commit suicide didn't do so. She should have realised he meant it. Gone to him after he had left her, sought him out in his apartment and said that she would do as he had suggested. She would live with him as his wife. And yes of course she was still in love with him, and always would be. They must forget about the previous day that she had believed had been her wedding-day till his legal wife had so shatteringly proved that she was wrong. They must start again. As she had said to him she was his wife. To her he was her husband.

But she couldn't do that now. It was too late. His life was on her conscience. It would be for the rest of *her* life. This was something from which she would never recover.

She scarcely slept that night. In the morning she knew she could bear her apartment no longer. Not for a while at any rate. She must get away. Besides friends might try to contact her, might feel they should do something about her if they read the news story of Hank's suicide and her own part of it in the papers.

She packed a suit-case and went down in the elevator. Joe was in the foyer. He looked at her anxiously, his dark eyes full of sympathy.

"I'm going away for a few days, Joe."

"Yes, Miss Duke."

"I don't want any mail forwarded."

"Okay. Take care of yourself."

"I'll be all right."

She blessed him for his reticence. She had been a little afraid that he might have made some reference to the tragedy.

She took a taxi to Grand Central Station and a ticket to Lakeville in Connecticut. She had once spent a week with friends there. They had taken her to dinner at a lakeside hotel and she had thought how peaceful it was and how beautiful.

She only had a short while to wait for a train. She found a corner seat and tried to make her mind a blank. She wasn't Linda Duke. She was someone quite different. A girl going off for a few days' holiday.

At the first station a man got out leaving

behind him a newspaper. She didn't want to look at it and yet she had to. As she had feared, there on the front page were pictures of Hank and herself. And beneath hers "Linda Duke, the girl Hank Nickson loved. The girl because of whom he shot himself."

The photograph was a shockingly bad reproduction of the one Hank had had on his bedside table. She had thought it good at the time, so had he. But in this rag of a newspaper and from the news story beneath it she might be a veritable toughie, a girl without a conscience who would steal any woman's husband. She was glad it wasn't the sort of paper anyone who knew her would be likely to read. Or was that wishful thinking?

She was thankful when at last she reached Lakeville. Here there was quiet though now that she had left the bustling noisy city she was by no means sure it had been the wisest move. In Lakeville there were no distractions. The hotel had few visitors. But the surroundings were very beautiful. It was a little New England town with its white houses and neat green lawns fronting them.

But as the days passed the agony she was suffering didn't lessen. It was with her every waking moment of every day and haunted her dreams at night. Hank was dead. She had killed him. No, that was absurd. She mustn't allow herself to think this. But he had warned her what he would do and she hadn't believed he meant it. She should have shown more understanding, more sensitivity.

There were times when she thought she couldn't bear it. That she must do as he had done. And then she knew of course she wouldn't. She wouldn't be so cowardly. She had her mother and Piers and Sarah to consider. Besides she was young. This agony of mind would pass. Time healed all things. That might be trite but please God it must be true.

At the end of a fortnight she felt no better. If possible the pain was even more acute. It was as if she were coming round from an operation, the surgeon was still operating and there was no anaesthetic.

At the beginning of the third week she returned to New York. She was still uncertain what she wanted to do, get a job she supposed and the sooner the better and, as she had been vaguely considering, perhaps one in a quite different part of the States. She might somehow force herself to start life anew though she rather doubted it.

Her apartment was dusty and depressing with, understandably, a neglected feeling about it. When first she had moved in she had been thrilled with it but not any more. Now it held only painful memories for her. She flung open the windows and began vigorously to clean it, polishing the furniture, vacuuming the carpets, cleaning what little bits of silver she had.

She looked at her desk, thinking what a chaotic muddle it was in whereas usually she kept it so tidy. She sat down before it to restore order. She glanced idly through the pigeon holes and saw her mother's last letter. She read it again. "How are you, darling? We all miss you very much though I perhaps more than the other two. It seems so long since you went to New York. I wish you would come home, even if only for a holiday."

Home. She knew now what she would do. She would go home. And not for a holiday, she would go for good. She would never return to New York. She would never be able to bear it.

It was a relief to have come to a decision. She washed, re-did her face, picked up her bag and gloves and went down in the elevator and to the nearest tourist office.

"I want to book a flight to London, please," she said to the pleasant-faced girl who came forward to know what she could do for her.

"How soon do you want it?"

"As soon as possible."

The girl smiled.

"Something tells me you don't like New York."

"New York's all right, but not for me."

"This your first visit?"

"It's more than a visit. I've been here nearly three years. But now I'm anxious to go home."

The girl consulted some timetables. The planes were heavily booked, she said. A lot of Americans liked to go to England at this time of the year.

"Fancy a Jumbo? They're very comfortable."

Linda was nervous of flying. She knew it was stupid, everyone flew these days, but she couldn't help it. She suffered agonies of fear at take-off and landing and never felt entirely at ease even when airborne.

"I think I'd rather go on a Boeing."

"Okay. I can fix you up for the day after tomorrow. Eight o'clock from Kennedy Airport. You need to check in by seven-thirty. The coach leaves from the Airways Terminal an hour before."

The day after tomorrow. It seemed to Linda almost too good to be true. She paid for her ticket, put it safely away in her wallet, thanked the girl and left the Tourist Agency to look for an American Express. She sent her mother a cable "Arriving Heathrow 20.00. Thursday. Feeling fine but suddenly longing to see you all. Love. Linda."

She put in that she was feeling fine in case the cable worried her mother. It would be a surprise for her family. A pleasant one she hoped. For the first time since the tragedy of Hank she began to feel just a little better. It would be wonderful to be home. Her mother and she were very close. They always had been. But she wouldn't tell her mother what had happened. She could tell no one. She was afraid her mother would guess something was wrong to bring her back so unexpectedly but she wouldn't ask questions. She was that kind of mother. Linda thought how lucky she was to have her.

She went to the agents from whom she had got her apartment and said she was returning to England unexpectedly and wished to sublet it. The girl looked at her curiously. Linda guessed she knew why she was leaving New York.

"There'll be no difficulty in that, Miss Duke. We have a long waiting list. Accommodation is hard to get in this city."

"It is in London too," said Linda and thought how lucky she was to have a home to go to.

She packed her cases, checked the inventory of her apartment with the clerk the agency sent who congratulated her on the way she was leaving it and the fact that she had broken nothing.

"I'm fairly careful."

"More than most tenants are. You should see some of the places I am sent to."

When the man had gone she caught sight of herself in a mirror and decided something needed to be done about her appearance. She looked old and haggard or so she thought. But maybe a hair-do and a facial might improve matters.

She didn't go to her usual hair salon. The girl who did her hair there doubtless knew what had happened. She chose one where she was a stranger. She decided to have a manicure too.

"What colour would you like?" asked the manicurist.

Linda didn't care. She glanced disinterestedly at the array of bottles, picking up first one and then another. Love-Mist. Jewelled Glory. What absurd names! Broken Heart. She wouldn't have thought that would be very popular. Except for her.

"I'll have this one," she said, sharp tears pricking her eyes.

She looked better when she paid her bill and caught sight of her reflection. She assuredly had needed to. Now perhaps her family wouldn't think there was anything much wrong with her. After all, they would expect her to be tired after the flight.

Joe took her cases down to the taxi for her the following morning.

"I'm sure sorry to see you go, Miss

Duke," he said as he shook her warmly by the hand.

She pressed a hundred-dollar bill into his, insisting he must take it when he tried to refuse.

"You've been a good friend to me, Joe."

"It's been swell having you here. You're different from most of the tenants."

She checked in at the airport and waited for her flight to be called. She could hardly believe that soon now she would be in England. A few hours and the giant plane should touch down at Heathrow. Would her family be there to meet her? She thought it most likely. Unless of course they were away. The possibility of this appalled her. But supposing they had gone off on a family holiday and there had only been dear old Annie at home when her cable had arrived?

But no, that surely was unlikely. Anyway, her mother rarely took a holiday. Linda used to try to persuade her to but she always insisted she was too busy. She couldn't leave her patients.

"Will the passengers on flight four-three-five proceed to gate seven."

She had her passport and ticket ready

and her boarding pass. An air stewardess shepherded her fellow passengers and herself to the plane. There was no bus to take them to it. They walked straight down the covered passage into the cabin. This she had never done before. When she had flown out to the States there had been steps to go up at Heathrow.

The plane was only half-full. There was no other passenger sitting beside her for which she was relieved. She would hate to have been with someone who insisted on talking as had happened when she had flown over from England. A garrulous American woman, hearing she was going to New York for the first time, had insisted on telling her all she must see and do. It had seemed to Linda that she hadn't stopped chattering for a single moment.

She fastened her seat-belt and leaned back. She heard the doors close and the whine of the jets. She wished she didn't feel so absurdly nervous. But she felt so shut in. She couldn't escape if she tried.

The plane was backing now, then turning and crossing the tarmac to the runway. There it stopped. The whine of the jets increased till it reached a deafening crescendo. There was silence among the passengers. She had noticed on the way out that no one spoke much at take-off and landing. She glanced around her. Perhaps these apparently unconcerned other passengers weren't as calm as they looked. The plane gathered speed, the airport buildings were rushing past, faster, faster, then she realised that they had left the ground and were rapidly gaining height. In no time at all she was looking out of the window at her side down on New York. There was the Hudson and the East rivers, the Empire State Building, Central Park, all the familiar landmarks.

She was conscious of a medley of emotions. Misery because of the tragedy that had engulfed her, relief that she was leaving all associations with it behind. Soon she would be home. Her cold heart warmed faintly. She made up her mind never to cross the Atlantic again.

Now they were passing through clouds and were once again in brilliant sunshine with blue skies. The plane was steady as a rock. The red light over the door leading to the flight deck was extinguished. Seat-belts were being discarded, cigarettes lighted.

A stewardess came along with a tray of bottles. Linda had a brandy. Lunch the stewardess said would be served shortly. She had had no breakfast. She had in fact scarcely eaten anything since she had returned from Lakeville and she had had no appetite there. The head waiter at the hotel had said she didn't eat enough to keep a sparrow alive. She supposed she should make a determined effort to eat some lunch.

She looked far down to the ocean. How calm the sea was! She was lucky to have such a smooth flight.

The hours passed and now she saw land below, green fields and little villages. The stewardess told her they were passing over Ireland.

"We'll be in on time," she said. "You've been lucky. This is the first really smooth flight we've had for some days. Yesterday the passengers were continually being told to fasten their seat-belts and extinguish their cigarettes there was so much turbulence."

"I'm glad there hasn't been today."

She looked down on the Irish Channel and saw now the English coastline. At last she was flying over her own country. She felt a wave of affection for it. People might knock England but she loved it. She longed for London with its graceful buildings and charm. Her mother had told her in a recent letter that she imagined it must be growing increasingly like America, there were so many sky-scraper buildings being erected, but even so Westminster Abbey, St. Paul's, all the landmarks she remembered so well would still be there.

"I wish you would tell me what happened. It might help to talk about it. If one is desperately unhappy it sometimes does, you know."

She started at Dirk's voice. The past vanished and she was back in the present. She was in David's consulting-room and Dirk was looking down at her. She looked at him in bewilderment. With a trembling hand she pushed her hair back from her forehead. Could it really only have been a few moments since he had asked her for her side of the story?

She sat back in her chair feeling drained of all emotion. She wished she could sleep. Sleep and never wake up. Never be forced again to remember.

"Do you really want to hear it?" she asked.

"Yes."

"Will you believe it if I tell you? Haven't you already made up your mind about me?"

"I thought I had, I'll admit. Now I am not so sure. I have an idea I could have misjudged you."

"I wonder what is making you think that?"

"The way you look. The way you are. The sound of your voice. My own perception."

Her eyes hardened.

"Suppose you tell me first just what you have heard about me."

"I have already done so. I believed you took Hank Nickson away from his wife. I believed that when Hank died you intended to hold on to his money. Please forgive me for being so frank but you did ask me. Now won't you tell me your version of what happened?"

Linda hesitated. She dreaded having to tell him. She had already just relived it in her mind. It would be agony to go into it all again. She had to force herself to begin.

She told him of her first meeting with Hank that weekend on Long Island and all that had resulted from it. Occasionally she omitted certain things but she felt she owed this to Hank. But she told Dirk all that really mattered. When at last her story was finished he was silent for several minutes. The grandfather clock ticked noisily. There was the distant murmur of traffic. The sound of a dog barking. The front-door bell ringing and Whitlock crossing the hall to answer it.

At last Dirk said, "Thank you for telling me. I'm afraid you found it very painful."

"I did. It brought it all back. I've been trying so hard to forget."

"Now you must."

"It's not going to be easy." She pressed her fingers to her throbbing temples. Her nerves felt stretched. Another moment and she would scream which would be ridiculous and out of character. Usually she was so composed. In trouble, and God knew she had been in trouble recently, she turned in upon herself. She looked up at Dirk. "Why did you do this to me? It was cruel of you." Now all her resentment against him flared again. "Why couldn't you have left me alone? I told you last time we met what you wanted to know. I had no idea Hank had left me his money and I wouldn't touch a penny of it. His wife could have it all. Please cable her and tell her so at once." She looked at him, her brows drawn together. "How do you come into this, anyway? Are you in love with Hank's wife? Is that why you are going to such lengths to see that she gets his money?"

Dirk flinched. He deserved this he supposed. It was only understandable that Linda should want to hit back. All the same she was glad she had hurt him. Why should it all be one-sided?

"No, I'm not in love with Kate," Dirk said. "In fact I hardly know her. I have only met her a few times. But I saw the news story. It gave a very false picture of you. I wrote to Kate to say how shocked I was to hear of Hank's death. At that time I was in Chicago. I thought she wasn't going to answer my letter then she wrote asking me if I was in New York at any time if I would go to see her. She told me she was in desperate financial straits and that you had been left all Hank's money."

Linda said dully, "I didn't know Hank had so much money."

"Oh yes, he was quite a wealthy man. I take it you didn't know very much about him?"

"I knew very little. We met only a few weeks before —" she hesitated — "before we, as I believed, married. As I told you no one was at our wedding. Two strangers were our witnesses. This was the way Hank wanted it and as my family were here in England and I had no real friends in New York that suited me too. It never occurred to me that he could have had a reason for wanting it to be kept so quiet."

"It wouldn't," Dirk smiled and shook his head, "you're the trusting sort, aren't you, Linda?"

"I'm a great deal more than that," she said bitterly, "I'm also gullible and a fool."

"I wouldn't say that. Hank had terrific charm."

Linda didn't wish to be reminded of it.

"It's odd I haven't heard about the money yet."

"Not really. These things always take time. Don't forget the lawyer had to track you down. Kate said he was being very dilatory about it. I saw her on my way through New York and as soon as she knew I was coming to London she begged me to try to contact you. She said she thought it very likely you had returned to your family who lived in Wimbledon. Someone she had run into who had known you had told her this."

"I wonder who that could have been?"

"I've no idea. But she begged me to try to contact you and to ask you at least to continue giving her the allowance Hank had given her."

Linda said, "It staggers me that he believed he could get away with" — she hesitated — "it's such a hideous word but there is no other — bigamy."

"I guess he hoped to. But Hank was like that. He took what he wanted from life regardless of the effect it might have on other people. And to be fair a divorce was pending and Kate changed her mind at the last moment. She admitted this much. He had been trying to persuade her to set him free for some time."

"I can't understand any woman wanting to hold on to a man if he is no longer in love with her."

"You wouldn't, of course, but Kate's different. And she had a hell of a time with Hank almost from the word go. Personally I would have thought she would have considered herself well rid of him. I suppose the truth was she didn't want him herself but didn't want any other woman to have him. And I think once she realised how desperately anxious he was that some other woman should, she turned her toes in."

"But surely even so Hank could have got a divorce? I thought it was so easy in the States, that if one or other was determined to put an end to a marriage there was no problem."

"It's not quite as simple as that. Different states have different laws. I expect he would have got one in the end but Hank didn't want to wait. He was always impatient."

Linda refused to allow fresh memories to awaken. But Dirk was right, of course. How often Hank had said he wanted her so desperately that he couldn't wait till they were married, that in this day and age it was senseless to, no one did. She had been tempted to agree but somehow she hadn't been able to bring herself to. She supposed that had been why he had rushed her into what she had believed to have been their marriage.

"I still don't know how you tracked me down," she said. "Oh yes, we met at that drinks party at the Morrisons' but surely that was the most astonishing coincidence?"

"Actually it wasn't. Kate knew a little about you. Apparently after you left the St. Regis there was one hell of a row between her and Hank. I didn't get any details but my bet is she traduced you up hill and down dale and called you a slut and everything else that was unpleasant. He, infuriated by the way she was carrying on, flung back at her that you were an English girl and that your family lived in London. Then she ran into that girl who knew you. Now I come to think of it I believe her name was Susan something or other."

That would have been Susan Parker who had married and gone to California. In her last letter she had said she hoped shortly to be coming to New York for a few days and then they must meet.

"I know now who you mean," Linda said. "She was a girl I shared an apartment with till she married and went to live on the West Coast."

She could imagine the scene that had taken place between Hank and his wife. She could see again the other woman, white faced, stony eyed, her voice like a two-edged sword. She wouldn't have spared Hank. Neither, Linda imagined, would Hank have spared her.

She brought herself back to the present. "Yes, Hank knew about Mother, and my brother and sister. Naturally I had told him about them. We had planned to come to England together so that I could introduce him to them. We — "

She couldn't go on. Dirk's hand covered hers.

"Linda dear, don't think about it any more. Can't you look upon your stay in New York, your meeting with Hank and all that happened after, as a chapter in your life that is now closed?"

"I want to."

"You must. Incidentally you asked me how I found you. When I arrived in London I looked through all the Dukes in the telephone book." He smiled. "And believe me there are quite a number. Your mother however has ‘physiotherapist’ after her name. It seemed a bit much to call you up and say I wanted to see you. When we did meet I hadn’t decided how I would set about it. You must remember I had no idea what you were really like.”

Linda looked at him, her face white, her eyes full of suffering.

“You expected to find me a hard-boiled husband-snatcher. You imagined you could easily have difficulty in getting me to agree to Hank’s wife having some of his money?”

“I’m afraid I did. But you must admit that was hardly my fault. Our actual meeting was, I agree, a coincidence but those sort of coincidences often happen in life. Friends in New York gave me an introduction to the Morrisons. I called them up and they asked me along for drinks that evening. In passing Mrs. Morrison said that your mother, who was her masseuse, was there and she introduced me to her. Your mother told me that her daughter who had recently returned from New York was calling for her. I thought my luck was in. That it must be you. That it would be a perfectly natural way for me to meet you.”

"As it was."

"Yes. And you took a very obvious and immediate dislike to me."

"I'm sorry. But you know why."

"I certainly do. But you turned out to be totally different from what I expected." His eyes searched her face. "Will you believe me if I tell you that I am terribly sorry? I truly want to apologise most humbly."

"There's no need to. Just forget it."

He looked down at her.

"I can't. Unless you agree that from now on we can be friends."

She shrugged.

"Please, Linda — "

She said desperately, "I don't know, Dirk. You knew Hank. You know about me. All that happened. I don't think I ever want to see anyone connected with that terrible time again. And if I see you — "

Dirk took her hands.

"Listen, Linda. All this has been a nightmare for you. You are afraid it will always be a nightmare and you will never wake up. But you are wrong. You're young, you're lovely, you still have your life before you. And one day — " He hesitated. "No, maybe that had better wait, but one day there is a great deal I am going to say to you. For the time being — will you have dinner with me this evening?"

"I don't know. Why are you asking me?"

"Because I want to get to know you better. And because there is nothing I would rather do than spend the evening with you."

Linda hesitated. She glanced at the time. It was far later than she had believed possible. David would be returning any moment. Heaven knew what she must look like after such a storm of tears. She didn't want him to see that she had been crying.

At that moment the telephone bell rang. She lifted the receiver.

"Linda?" said David's voice. "I'll not be along again today. Tell Whitlock that, will you, and be off as soon as you like."

"Yes, David."

"You all right?"

"Yes, thank you."

She replaced the receiver.

"That was David."

"So I thought." Dirk smiled. "Still angry with him for making it easy for me to see you?"

She shook her head.

"No. Perhaps I needed to tell someone about what happened."

"I think you did. But that's all in the past. No more dwelling on it."

"I'll try not to."

"I'm not going to let you. Now — do anything you need to do here and then let's go."

It was her turn to smile.

"I'll have to tidy up first." She glanced at herself in a mirror. "I look terrible. I always do if I cry. Mercifully I don't very often."

He raised her chin with his fingertips so that he could look down directly into her eyes.

"You're not going to again for a long while," he said decisively, "if I have anything to do with it."

13

SARAH was lunching with Sue Alsop, another of the trainees at *Amanda's* Beauty Parlour. Sue was two years older than Sarah and had almost finished her training. Sarah had met Garry at a party Sue had given.

"Only a fortnight now and I'm off on holiday," said Sarah.

"Lucky girl. I have to wait till September. Have you decided yet where you are going?"

"Yes," said Sarah, looking dreamily into space. The sun was shining, the sky was blue and there were stretches of golden sands. Garry and she were strolling along beside a sparkling sea, his arm round her shoulders. It was all idyllic. They were so much in love. They were making plans for when he was free and they could marry.

"Where are you going?" asked Sue.

"Down to Cornwall."

"With your family?"

Sarah shook her head. "Not on your life."

Sue looked at Sarah interestedly. Sarah was such a romantic little thing. And so gullible. She just hadn't got her feet on the ground. In fact Sue considered Sarah a fool in many ways. She had an uneasy feeling that she might be considering making an even bigger fool of herself than she had already.

"Don't tell me you're going off on holiday with Garry?"

"I am."

"You must be joking."

"Indeed I'm not."

"Then you're crazy," said Sue flatly.

Sarah resented this. How dare Sue criticise her? What had it to do with her anyway?

"Why am I crazy?" she asked coldly.

"Because friend Garry is leading you up the garden path and if you had any sense you would realise it."

Sarah told herself angrily that the trouble with Sue was she was jealous. A friend of Garry's had taken him to the party at Sue's, where they had met and it had been she, Sarah, Garry had fallen for and not Sue. In fact he had told her afterwards that he thought Sue a bore and not in the least attractive.

"I don't know why you should say that. Maybe you'll change your opinion when I tell you that Garry and I are going to be married. He's divorcing his wife as soon as it can be arranged."

Sue stared at Sarah and decided she was an even bigger fool than she feared.

"He's not really tried to make you believe that, has he?"

"It's true." Sarah's voice rose indignantly. "Why are you so horrible about him?"

"I'm not horrible. I'm just trying to tell you a few home truths. My darling Sarah, Garry's not in the least likely to divorce his wife. He may try to kid you that he is but you can take it from me it's not true. For one thing his wife has quite a bit of money and Garry finds that very useful. I know a great deal more about him than you do."

Sarah's cheeks flamed. It was the first she knew of Garry's wife having any money. And if it were true she was quite sure that wouldn't prevent Garry from going ahead with a divorce. Besides why should it? He was a very successful PRO. Oh yes, she knew occasionally he was a bit short of cash, but then he was very generous. And as he had said to her, occasionally he had to wait for money that was due to him.

"I think that's a perfectly dreadful thing to say," she said angrily.

Sue shrugged.

"Sorry. But I assure you if his wife hadn't quite a bit of money he would often be in one hell of a jam. Incidentally she's almost as big a fool about him as you are."

"That I know isn't true. They fight like cat and dog."

"So do plenty of married couples but that doesn't mean they're going to end up in the divorce courts.

Sarah shrugged.

"Have it your own way. But don't say I didn't warn you."

Sarah said furiously, "Your trouble is you're jealous because I'm the one Garry fell for at your party and not you."

Sue laughed good-temperedly. "Don't be ridiculous. I've no more time for Garry than he has for me. But I'm fond of you,

Sarah, and I think the sooner you come to your senses about him the better. Still it's nothing to do with me. Look, we'd better get our bill or we'll be late back and then we'll be in the dog-house. We're cram full of the idle rich this afternoon wanting to be made beautiful."

Sue's words rankled with Sarah for the remainder of her working day. She found it hard to concentrate on her job. Usually she enjoyed it. It interested her to see a woman come into *Amanda's* looking tired and lined and going out an hour or so later looking years younger and very much happier.

Sharp at half-past five she went to the cloakroom. She was meeting Garry at a little nearby bar at a quarter to six. She re-did her face and ran a comb through her hair.

"You look very nice," said Sue's voice behind her.

Sarah turned. "Thanks."

Sue smiled. "Still sore at me?"

"No, but you were rather horrid at lunch."

"You know why. However — good luck. Have a nice evening. I don't need to ask who you're meeting. You needn't give him my love."

Sarah called good-bye to the other girls and hurried out of *Amanda's*. It was the rush hour and the streets were crowded with people anxious to get away from their various shops and offices.

Sue's harsh words about Garry were still rankling when she reached the bar where they were to meet. She glanced around as she entered it but there was no sign of him. A couple of men looked at her with interest. She was used to men eyeing her. It often happened. According to her mood she felt flattered or indignant. To-night she felt indignant. She was annoyed with Garry for being late. When after twenty minutes he eventually arrived with only a brief apology she felt a rising resentment.

"I was held up just as I was leaving the office," he said. He beckoned the waiter and ordered a sherry for Sarah and a large whisky for himself.

"I think I'd rather have a gin and French," said Sarah.

"Well, you're not going to, my pretty one. Gin and French isn't for little girls."

Sarah bristled. "I'm not a little girl."

Garry chuckled. "To me you are."

She could have hit him.

The waiter brought the drinks and set the glasses before them.

"Here's luck," said Garry.

"Here's to our holiday."

Garry sighed and wondered whether to break the news to Sarah right away that he was afraid the holiday they had planned wasn't after all going to be possible or to wait till later in the evening. He had been a fool, of course, to have led her to believe it would be possible. But at the time he had suggested it he had thought Emma was going off on a cruise with her friend Muriel and he had seen no reason why she would change her mind. But Emma, unpredictable at all times, had told him at breakfast that morning that her plans were altered. She didn't want to go away with Muriel. In fact she would far prefer a holiday with him and why didn't the two of them go off somewhere together?

Garry could have given her a very good reason why he hadn't thought much of this idea. The main one being that he had already made other plans. But Emma and he miraculously seemed to have been getting on rather better recently. It was in fact quite a while since they had had one of their first-class rows. And last week Emma had helped him out with a cheque for a bill that had been pressing. He had promised to let her have it back at the end of the month but she had told him airily not to worry. She had had some dividends in the previous week so she was all right for money.

It was a pity that money, or rather the lack of it, played such an important part in so many people's lives. He supposed he was bad at managing his. He always had been. It would have been impossible to have married Emma if she hadn't had money of her own. She was as extravagant as he was but she could afford to be.

Sarah looked at him and her rancour vanished as she remembered how very much she was in love with him.

"I'm so longing to get away, Garry," she said softly. "Just think — we've never been on our own together for more than a few hours. To be just the two of us for a whole fortnight will be heaven."

Garry doubted it. He had the uneasy

feeling that a fortnight of Sarah swooning with love for him could prove a little irritating. And he thought as he had thought quite a few times recently that really he should break with her. In fact if he had any sense he would do this and try to make a go of things with Emma. It would be far fairer both to Emma and to Sarah.

He finished his drink and ordered the same again.

Sarah edged her chair a little nearer to his. She slid her hand into his.

"You do love me, don't you, Garry? I mean as much as ever?"

Garry patted her hand and said he supposed so.

"Only suppose?"

Garry looked at her. He was rather glad the bar had so few other customers because Sarah had such a glowing, hopeful expression on her face that he found it almost embarrassing.

"Look, sweetie, couldn't we get through just one evening without you wanting to know how much I love you?"

"I'd rather not."

"But don't you realise that a man doesn't

want to have to reassure a girl continually?"

"But I like you to."

"I find it a bit monotonous."

"I don't. And I never will. You couldn't tell me too often."

Garry sighed. Sarah was beginning to bore him. And not for the first time.

"Look, put back that drink and let's go and have some food. I only had a sandwich for lunch and I'm getting hungry."

Sarah finished her sherry obediently.

"Where shall we go?" she asked as they left the bar.

"Let's go to that little restaurant on the Embankment where we've been so often before."

Sarah didn't really mind much where they went. It was enough for her that they were together. But she wished Garry wouldn't be so tetchy. Maybe he had had a difficult day at his job. He had often told her his work was very exacting. She had better bear this in mind and be sweet as honey, not say anything provocative that might irritate him.

They took a bus to Chelsea and down Oakley Street to the Embankment.

Sarah slid her hand through Garry's arm. "Let's walk along by the river for a few minutes before we have dinner." And as they did this, "Not long now, darling, and we'll have that whole fortnight together. Just imagine it. I won't have to go back to my home and you won't have to go back to yours."

Garry decided the time had come for him to tell her the truth. It couldn't be delayed any longer.

"I'm afraid, my pretty one, that's all been a pipe-dream. I'm terribly sorry but the holiday we had planned just isn't possible."

Sarah stopped dead and stared at him speechlessly.

"Why not?" she asked at last.

"Because I won't be able to get away from the office. My boss is going at that particular time."

"But surely you haven't just discovered that?"

"Actually I have. He should have gone later but he's switched his holiday."

Garry wondered why he was bothering to lie to Sarah. And knew he was a coward. He was trying to take the easy way out.

He didn't feel at all proud of himself. But then he hadn't for some while now regarding Sarah, or Emma either for that matter.

Sarah told herself it couldn't be true. He was teasing her. Only it was rather ill-timed teasing. She wasn't in any mood for it this evening.

"I'm damned sorry, Sarah darling, but it isn't my fault."

Sarah didn't believe him. "But I thought it was all arranged? We've been planning it for weeks." Her eyes filled with tears and her lips trembled. "Garry, you can't do this to me. You just can't."

Garry sighed. "Unfortunately, I must. Actually there's another reason why I can't be out of town at the time we planned. I had thought Emma was going off on a cruise with a girl-friend but she's changed her mind."

At the mention of his wife's name Sarah saw red.

"What difference does that make?"

"Sarah, be reasonable. How can I be away for a couple of weeks unless Emma goes off somewhere too?"

"But why shouldn't you? You're free to do as you like."

"Not yet."

"You're going to be very shortly." And now Sarah was remembering Sue's words of warning at lunch. She heard her again telling her that in her opinion Garry was leading her up the garden path, and even more wounding, that she was a fool if she believed Garry was going to divorce his wife, his wife who, according to Sue, was as crazy about him as she was. She hadn't believed Sue could possibly be right. Why, from the very beginning Garry had told her that Emma and he fought like cat and dog and each was only too anxious to be free of the other. But Sue had said that plenty of married couples fought but it didn't mean they ended up in the divorce courts.

Could it possibly be that Garry had never had any intention of breaking with his wife?

"If, as you've led me to believe, you and your wife are getting a divorce, why can't you go off on holiday any time you like? What can it matter to her where you go or what you do?"

Garry felt his temper rising. "I don't want to be ungallant but you have done more talking about this divorce of mine than ever I have."

Sarah gasped. "That's not true."

"Indeed it is, my pretty one. And if you weren't given to refusing to face facts you would know it."

"That's another lie. You've always led me to believe right from the start that soon you would be free. You're not suggesting I imagined it, are you?"

"Well, I'd say you have a pretty lively imagination. Anyway, maybe I felt like it the day you and I met. Doubtless Emma and I had had one hell of a row. We often do. Maybe we always will but that doesn't mean we're going to end up in the divorce courts."

Sarah could have screamed. Sue's very words. Sue who obviously was far more knowledgeable about men than she was.

Garry added fuel to the fire. "The thing is, however fierce our rows are, we always somehow manage to make them up again."

"You — you utter heel!"

Garry chuckled. "Go ahead, call me anything you like if it makes you feel any better. Actually, to be honest, there have been times when I, too, have thought I was a bit of a heel. I'm not attempting to whitewash myself, darling. I suppose if I were honest I'd admit that I have treated both you and Emma badly."

"Badly!" Sarah's voice rose hysterically. "You've broken my heart, you've ruined me, you — "

Garry decided this was a bit too much. "Listen here, I have *not* ruined you. Mind you, that wasn't your fault and I won't deny that nothing would have given me greater pleasure. But somehow — " He shook his head. "Perhaps I'm not such a heel after all. Many men would have done. Though in this day and age it's a somewhat old-fashioned way of putting it."

Sarah couldn't believe this was Garry talking. Not the Garry she loved and would willingly have followed to the ends of the earth. She looked at him out of brimming eyes and suddenly saw him as someone quite different. This Garry she hated.

"You're despicable," she said bitterly. "I can't think why I ever imagined myself in love with you. Thank God I've come to my senses. I'm sorry for the next girl you try to seduce. I — "

She couldn't go on.

Garry put back his head and roared with laughter. "Sarah, you're marvellous. You've missed your vocation. You should have gone on the stage. For your information you were the one who did the seducing. Or at least more than your fair share of it. On consideration I'm not sure I shouldn't have been highly commended for having withstood you, for if ever a girl pursued a man — "

He got no farther. Sarah raised her hand and gave him a stinging blow across the cheek. Two people coming towards them looked at them with interest. Then she burst into tears, much to Garry's embarrassment.

"For God's sake stop it!" he flung at her furiously.

"I can't. I feel too awful. I hate you. I wish I'd never met you. I wish I were dead."

"You don't. You'd cling to life like a limpet. And if you don't stop making such an exhibition of yourself, I'm off. I can't stand scenes."

"I'll kill myself," screamed Sarah, believing for one wild moment that she meant it.

"Now, listen, stop behaving like a silly

little idiot and take my advice. What you need to do is to look around for someone else. Preferably a bachelor." As her sobs grew louder he felt increasingly exasperated. "And for God's sake, pull yourself together!"

"I can't," she stormed. "I swear to you I'll put my head in a gas oven and then you'll be sorry. Everyone will know how you've treated me. Including your wife. You'll never be able to hold up your head again."

She broke into a fresh torrent of sobbing. Garry felt if possible even more exasperated. He never could stand a woman in tears. He looked at her and was surprised to find that he wasn't in the least sorry for her. He might have been if she had taken it better when he had told her he was through with her. He forgave her for slapping his face which he felt was magnanimous of him but this outburst of hysteria was more than he could stomach.

"For God's sake stop bawling and let's call it a day with no hard feelings and we'll go and have something to eat."

"I'll never eat anything again," wailed Sarah.

Garry sighed. It seemed to him that he had been very long suffering. But he had had enough. He was only astonished that he had been so patient.

"OK, don't if you don't want to. And go and put your head in the first gas oven you can find. I tell you I don't care. But just take a word of advice. With the next man don't be quite so forthcoming and when it's over don't make such a hoo-ha about it. And above all else don't imagine you're in love and that he is too and that it is going to last for all time. Because it won't. It doesn't at your age nor, as I now know, does it at mine. Oh for the love of Mike . . ."

Garry could easily have slapped Sarah's face but he refrained. All the same as now she burst into a fresh torrent of tears he too lost his temper.

"You silly little fool," he stormed at her. "If I had any lingering feeling for you I haven't any longer. You're enough to drive any man up the wall. Maybe as you grow older you'll learn sense but you don't seem to have much at the moment. So now it's good-bye and I hope I don't cross your path again or you mine."

With this he turned quickly on his heel

and walked back up Oakley Street towards the King's Road.

Sarah stood and watched him. He didn't look back. And now she wasn't crying any more. In fact to her astonishment she was beginning to feel rather better. She told herself dramatically that a chapter in her life was closed and she was glad. It had been ill-fated from the start. She should have had more sense than to get involved with a married man. She was much too angry now to feel unhappy. She only hoped she would remain this way because it was so much more sensible.

She took her compact from her bag and looked at herself critically. It was unbecoming to cry. She looked awful but she knew from past experience that she could be in tears one moment and once they were over within a short while she looked all right again.

She saw a passing taxi and hailed it.

"Waterloo," she said to the driver.

She didn't often take taxis. She couldn't afford them. But she felt reckless. She would go home and call up Harriet and suggest that if she were free they went to a flick together.

And now as the taxi bowled along she

went over in her mind all that had passed between her and Garry and her fury mounted. The things they had said to each other! She could hardly believe it. He had certainly spared her no more than she had spared him. She was glad she had slapped his face. That made her one up on him. And he could hardly have slapped hers however much he might have wanted to. Looking back on the violence of their quarrel she supposed it had all been rather public. It had been a pity that it had taken place while they had been on the Embankment.

In the train on her way to Wimbledon she knew that there would be times no doubt when her anger against Garry would vanish and she would wish he was still in her life. But she hoped they would be infrequent and before long she would forget him.

She wished Sue hadn't been proved right about him. This she found hard to bear. She wondered if she need tell her that all was over between them. She would much prefer not to. It seemed to her now that she had been foolish to confide in Sue. But Sue had introduced her to Garry and it had been good to have someone to talk to about him.

But it would be less humiliating if she could let Sue believe it was she, Sarah, who had broken with Garry. She might even hint that it had been because of all Sue had said to her at lunch that day. It had influenced her. Thinking it over during the afternoon she had decided that maybe Sue had been right. So when she had met Garry in the evening she had insisted they shouldn't meet again. After all, he was married —

She felt rather better once she had decided on this.

She decided also that she would allow her mother to think so too. And her mother, once she knew, Sarah was sure would be relieved. And being her mother and always so understanding she would ask no embarrassing questions.

She phoned Harriet as soon as she reached home.

"Doing anything this evening?" she asked.

"No. Why? Are you?"

"No. I believe there's a good Western at the Odeon."

"Fine. Let's go. That is if you're really free."

"I am," and over her shoulder to Annie, "Is Mummy in?"

Annie said her mother had telephoned a few moments ago and said she wouldn't be in to dinner. Linda also had rung a few moments before to say she too would be out. Annie didn't know about Piers but Sarah didn't bother about him.

"Meet you in a quarter of an hour in the foyer," she said to Harriet.

"I'll be there. But how is it you aren't out with the boy-friend? I thought you said you were meeting him tonight."

"I was. But I'm not after all. I'll tell you when I see you, Harriet, but he got a bit much. You know."

Harriet said she knew. And you couldn't trust any man. She added that, from all she had heard of Garry, she thought Sarah was well rid of him.

"I am, believe me," said Sarah with feeling.

She said good-bye to Harriet, replaced the receiver and called out to Annie that she wouldn't be in to dinner.

"The lot of you out," said Annie,

appearing in the kitchen doorway. "What's happening to this family? And here am I with a nice steak and kidney pudding all reading and waiting for you."

"Give it to us tomorrow," said Sarah cheerfully.

She was on the point of leaving a message for her mother but decided on a note instead. She went to her mother's desk in the drawing-room.

"Darling Mummy," she wrote. "I'm off to the flicks with Harriet. I'll come back as soon as they're over.

"And this time it really is with Harriet.

"I'm not seeing Garry any more."

14

CATHERINE straightened her back and smiled at Lady Dornford.

"That's all for today, I think. Are you feeling better?"

"Much. I always am after one of your treatments."

Catherine took off her white overall. She was glad that her working day was over. It had been a strenuous one. But then they all were. It wasn't easy being a physiotherapist. Still, she supposed she was lucky to be such a successful one. She always had as many patients as she could cope with. The doctors were very good to her. They recommended her to their patients. Without this she couldn't have been so successful.

Lady Dornford was one of David's patients. It was through him she had become one of Catherine's. Catherine liked and admired her for the way she bore her aching bones and often wished she could do more to alleviate their pain. Some while ago David had operated on Lady Dornford. It looked as if the operation was a success. The hip joint he had replaced was satisfactory.

"Do have a drink, Mrs. Duke, before you go?" suggested Lady Dornford.

"I don't think I will this evening, thank you all the same."

"But it's the witching hour."

"Not yet for me. I've another patient."

Catherine hoped this was a pardonable lie. But she wanted to be gone. Gone before Lady Dornford began to talk about David.

"I saw Mr. Cullis this morning and he's delighted with the way the operation has turned out. So I might say am I. He says I'm doing marvellously."

"So you are."

"He's terribly attractive, isn't he?"

"Yes."

"I felt rather concerned about him today. He looked so tired. I expect like so many of the medical profession he works too hard. It has always surprised me that he hasn't remarried."

Catherine said a quick good-bye and fled. The butler saw her out. Lady Dornford was among the few of Catherine's patients who still employed one. He opened the door of her car for her.

"Not much of a night, madam," he said with old world courtesy.

"It certainly isn't."

It was grey and overcast with a chill wind blowing. Catherine turned into Hyde Park. As she reached the bridge over the Serpentine on an impulse she stopped, got out of the car, locked it and walked across the spacious green turf away from the noise of the traffic. There were times when she told herself she didn't like London. Not any more. And if she could live in the country she would far prefer to. But of course it was out of the question. She needed to earn her living and she certainly couldn't do so in the country. But she wished London hadn't changed so much in recent years. She disliked the tall buildings that seemed to be going up almost daily. The old landmarks even seemed to be changing. Piccadilly Circus wasn't as it used to be. She missed the flower-women with their colourful baskets. Instead there were hippies lounging about, young men with long hair and girls in trousers. She often found it difficult to decide which sex they were.

She supposed she was old-fashioned. She didn't want to move with the times. She walked on, her head bent, trying to sort out the problem that had been growing in magnitude in her mind these last few days.

Had she done right to break with David? It distressed her to hear Lady Dornford say he looked tired. It couldn't be much of a life for him living alone. A man needed a woman to care for him. And heaven knew if only she could salve her conscience over her children how gladly she would fill that role. But whom should she consider? And at last, surprisingly, she suddenly knew the answer. David and herself. Now she realised that she was being a sacrificial mother. Something that David when he had asked her to marry him had warned her not to be. He had said he didn't approve of them.

But did she? This was a question she had found difficult to answer.

But if she gave up their home and married David what would become of them? At first she had thought it would be simple. They would live with her and David. But Linda and Piers had said they didn't want to. And she was worried about Sarah. How could she marry David and leave them to fend for themselves? At least the older two. Sarah would be with her but even so —

And how long was she going to keep from them that she wasn't after all going to marry David? Already Sarah was beginning to question her. It wouldn't be long before Linda and Piers did too. And one thing was certain. Not one of them would want her to give up David for their sake.

She should have thought of this before. But at the time she had decided to break with David she had been so desperately anxious about all three of them. She hadn't been able to see the wood for the trees.

But now, this evening, walking through Kensington Gardens with dark skies overhead and a chill wind blowing she was becoming increasingly convinced that she had made the wrong decision. And with this conviction it was as if a heavy cloak lifted. She knew now that a day would come when Linda, Piers and Sarah would solve their problems. Like birds leaving the nest they would leave their home. If she didn't marry David she would be alone.

She knew too that she was far more deeply in love with David than she had realised, so deeply in love that she was facing up squarely to the fact that she couldn't live without him. She wondered how he now felt about her, for he too had been as deeply in love as she. Of this she was certain. They were different from Linda, Piers and Sarah. One didn't fall in love easily or lightly in middle age. She knew that with Linda it couldn't have been lightly, but she was still young. Though she doubtless didn't believe it a day would come when she would fall in love again.

She supposed she should face the fact that by now for David too there could be someone else. Someone who had caught him on the rebound. Though a couple of years her senior he looked remarkably young for his age, and he was extremely successful. He would make any woman an enviable husband.

Not that it mattered to her one iota that she would be financially secure married o him. She would be as deeply in love with him if he hadn't two pennies to rub together.

She walked on, her hands dug deep into the pockets of her coat, asking herself if she could go to him and say that she regretted having said she couldn't marry him; that she couldn't think how she had ever brought herself to, but as he knew it had only been because of Linda, Piers and Sarah. But now she had come to her senses. If he were still in love with her, if he still wanted to marry her then he would make her the happiest woman in the world.

She would tell him too that she hadn't come to this decision because of any change in her children's circumstances. Nothing had altered. They were still just as much worry to her but she was putting herself before her children, and far more important her very urgent need of David before everything. She was in love with him as she had never been in love before and wanted to marry him. She didn't want to live a celibate life any longer, she was over forty it was true but when she thought of her love for him she often felt twenty years younger.

She looked up and found that without realising it she had retraced her steps to her car. She unlocked it, got in and drove to the nearest call box. She dialled David's number, leaning against the side of the box, her heart hammering against her side.

There was no answer from the Harley Street number. She was surprised because she thought even if David hadn't been there Linda would have been. But perhaps she had left punctually though often she stayed on quite late when David had patients calling to see him.

She dialled his home. Mrs. Noakes, his elderly housekeeper, answered.

"Is Mr. Cullis in, Mrs. Noakes?"

"I'm sorry but he isn't home yet. I don't think he'll be back till later."

"Thank you."

She knew she couldn't go home and sit there waiting for the time to pass till she could call David again. She rang her home and Annie answered.

"I won't be home to dinner, Annie. Will you tell the others when they come in? Or if any of them are there I'll speak to them."

Annie said that none of them were at home.

"Linda phoned a little while ago to say that she wouldn't be in until ten. Piers is out at the moment and Sarah's come in and gone out again."

"What have you got for dinner, Annie?"

"There's a steak and kidney pudding waiting for all of you. But Piers said this morning he didn't know what time he'd be in. Looks as if I'll have to eat it myself."

Despite her distress of mind Catherine suggested she left some for Piers, and Sarah in case she hadn't eaten when she eventually appeared.

"I am sure she would phone you if she was going to eat out," Catherine said.

Annie's reply to this was a disapproving grunt. But Annie was always annoyed if the family changed their minds about meals at the last moment. Not that Catherine blamed her. It must be tiresome to cook dinner for a family who didn't come to eat it. Catherine knew that even she was probably in disgrace. She smiled affectionately as she replaced the receiver. Poor dear Annie! She really was very patient with them all and often they were very trying. It was her children though who were the worst offenders. It never seemed to occur to them that to ring up at the last minute to say they wouldn't be in to meals could be disconcerting. And this evening she, herself, was doing just that.

She frowned as she left the box. She hoped Sarah wasn't meeting Garry Gold yet thought in all probability that she was. But tonight she couldn't even bother about that problem. Uppermost in her mind was her love for David. She knew she couldn't go home until she had seen him.

To fill in time she went to a cinema but left it before the main feature was about to start. Nine o'clock Mrs. Noakes had said David would be in. At a quarter past she parked her car near his flat. And as she had been hoping and praying within a few minutes a taxi drew up and David, alone, got out, paid the man and turned to go inside.

Quick as lightning she was out of her car and hurrying after him. He was beside the lift as she reached it.

"David!"

"Catherine! It can't be!"

She smiled.

"It is. Can I come up and talk to you?"

"What a question!" And anxiously,

"You're all right? I mean you're not ill. The family — ?"

"We're all fine, David. But I just wanted to see you."

She saw the joy on his face and felt relief sweeping over her. She dared not think how she would have felt had it been different. And it would have been only what she would have deserved. She wouldn't have blamed him. Her heart shook at the thought that he might not have been so obviously glad to see her. For it had been she who had broken with him. Who had begged him to find someone else and forget her.

He let her into his flat. Mrs. Noakes who came daily had already left and they were alone.

"I've been waiting for you to come to me," he said gently, his hands on her shoulders. "Praying that you would, sometimes certain you couldn't stay away, at others sure that all you said to me that last time when we lunched together had already been final."

"It wasn't, darling. I discovered that today. I can't think why it has taken me so long."

"Thank God that you have come at last!"

"Quite suddenly this evening as I was walking across Kensington Gardens I knew I couldn't bear to live without you. Indeed I didn't want to. I needed you so desperately. I — "

He held her closely and kissed her. Then he put her from him, looking at her critically, anxiously.

"You're white and tired. Before we talk and we are going to — have you had any dinner?"

She smiled, remembering that she hadn't.

"No, I forgot about it."

"I thought so. Sit down and I'll get you something."

He had led her into the drawing-room and pushed her gently into a chair. She looked up at him, not wanting him to go out of the room even for a moment, not wanting any food anyway.

"Truly, David, I couldn't eat anything."

"That's what you think. But you are going to. And you are going to have a drink."

She waited, looking round her while he was gone. How well she knew this room! She had helped him choose the décor, the carpets and curtains and furniture. They had been together at an auction sale at Christie's when he had bought the pine corner cupboard. Her photograph, the only one in the room, was on the bureau by the window. It was an elegant room, a man's room with feminine touches. It held warmth and friendliness and comfort as their home when they chose it would one day hold warmth and friendliness and comfort.

He was back in a few minutes. He put a tray with cold chicken and salad on a table at her side and opened a bottle of champagne.

She smiled.

"Do you always entertain your unexpected guests so lavishly?"

"No, but you are very special."

"Darling!" She held out her hand to him and he took it. "I wonder what I have done to deserve you!"

"Nonsense. It's the other way round. Tell me, did you have any lunch?"

"A sandwich."

"Catherine, darling, you promised me you would look after yourself."

"Did you have any?"

"You bet. An excellent one at my club."

"Men are so different from women. Nothing puts them off their food. Not love anyway."

"In other words love is for men a thing apart 'tis woman's whole existence."

"It assuredly is."

"Not for me. You are my whole existence."

She looked at him, asking a question to which she already knew the answer.

"Did you think my decision to break with you was final?"

"No, but I didn't know how long it would be before you came to me."

"As I have done tonight."

"As you have done tonight, thank God."

"I came most diffidently. After all, I wouldn't have blamed you if you had finished with me for all time."

"Catherine, darling, as if that would have been possible."

She sighed. But it was a happy sigh.

"Eat up, sweetheart," David said. "Food is important. I can't have you with a nervous breakdown just as we are about to set off for our honeymoon."

She did as he told her. Then he removed the tray. He sat beside her on the sofa, his arm round her shoulders.

"I imagine things are better with your children? Otherwise you wouldn't be here with me."

She turned to him swiftly, facing him.

"They aren't. They are just the same. In fact if possible even worse. But I have decided the children must resolve their own problems. I need you too much to let them come between us. And what is more I am quite sure they wouldn't want me to."

She saw his face light up at her words. She was glad that she had come to him despite Linda, Piers and Sarah. She was entitled to live her own life. And David would realise how much he meant to her, that it wasn't because her family problems were solved that she had felt free to marry him.

"I'm devoted to my three as you know, David, but, darling, you come first. Or at least — " she hesitated, feeling for words, "It's so different, isn't it? I feel it is time they fended for themselves. I'll help them all I can. But I couldn't sacrifice you or myself for them."

David held her close and kissed her. Time slipped by but they didn't notice.

Catherine felt young again. Everything was all right between David and herself. It seemed to her that nothing else could possibly matter.

15

LINDA, Piers and Sarah were all in the drawing-room wondering anxiously what had become of their mother. It was getting on for half-past eleven and she was still out. Surely she must realise that they were growing anxious about her?

Linda, who had come in soon after the other two, had been told by Annie that her mother had telephoned earlier in the evening to say she would be out to dinner but she wouldn't be home late.

Sarah said, "I can't think why she doesn't phone us. It's a bit much to allow us to be here worrying ourselves sick about her."

Linda looked at Piers.

"What would happen if she had had an accident?"

"The police would have called us. For heaven's sake, Linda, let's cross our bridges when we come to them. There is probably some quite simple explanation as to why she isn't home yet."

But inwardly he was growing increa ingly anxious. It wasn't like his mother be out so late without sending through an word as to what was detaining her. If sh were delayed by a patient she would hav sent a message. But she rarely saw he patients late in the evening. She alway tried to make her last one so that she wa free to be home by around seven.

Against that she had called Annie to sa she wouldn't be in to dinner. He wondere what was the best thing to do. Start ringin the hospitals?

Linda went to the window and drew aside the curtains. She wished there wasn't this concern about her mother on this particular evening. She was feeling so much happier. As if a great weight had been lifted from her shoulders. Dirk and she had had dinner together and now she liked him as much as so short a while ago she had disliked him. They had found they had a great deal in common. They enjoyed the same kind of books and plays. They liked country walks and on Sunday they planned to go out of London for a long day together. She had been looking forward to returning home and greeting her mother with a smile instead of her usual gloom to which her mother must by now have become resigned.

She wondered how her mother had put up with her since she had returned from America. She must have been a very trying member of the family. In fact all three of them, Linda thought, must have been pretty hard to put up with recently. Sarah with her frequent tantrums, and Piers out of a job and apparently not making the slightest effort to get one. Oh yes, she knew he was hoping to make money by writing but she doubted if he would succeed. It wasn't an easy profession. Many people imagined they could write but when they tried they found they hadn't the talent.

She turned back into the room.

"I'm going to call David," she said.

Sarah frowned. "I'm not sure if you should. I've an idea they've had a row."

Linda stared at her. "Surely not?"

"I think they have."

"Whatever makes you say that?" asked Piers.

"Feminine intuition."

Piers said he didn't believe in it. But now he became even more uneasy. He had been wondering for some little while how thing were going between his mother and David It was quite a time since David had beeı to the house and his mother hadn't men tioned him recently. He wondered wha could have gone wrong. He was sure Davic and his mother were deeply in love. O they certainly had been. And if they weren't any more —

Could it be possibly be that Linda, Sarah and he were responsible if there were a break between them ? The thought of this appalled him. Especially after all she had done for them.

"Even if you're right, Sarah, and they have I'm going to call David," said Linda. And when, after a few moments she returned to the drawing-room, "No reply from his number." She looked at her brother and sister. "I must admit I really am beginning to feel extremely worried."

Sarah looked from Linda to Piers, her eyes wide with anxiety. "Can't we do something ? We can't just sit here all night waiting for her to come in. Honestly, mothers can be a worry."

"How about their children being a

worry?" suggested Piers. "I've an idea all three of us have given her a bad time these past few weeks."

Sarah fought against an outburst of tears. She was growing more and more anxious every moment. The pleasant surprise her note should have given her mother had fallen flat. There it still lay on the desk waiting to be opened.

Suddenly they all rushed to the door as they heard a car stopping outside the house.

"It's Mummy and David," shouted Sarah who reached it first.

Catherine hurried towards them, holding Sarah close as her younger daughter flung herself into her arms.

"Mummy, Mummy, we thought you were dead," she sobbed.

Linda said, "We didn't, but we have been worried, Mother."

"Darlings, I'm terribly sorry. I should have phoned you. I tried a short while ago but the number was engaged so I thought it would be better to come straight home."

Linda smiled. "That must have been when I was calling David. I thought he might know where you were."

Catherine smiled at David over her shoulder.

"You were right. He did. But let's go along in."

In the drawing-room Catherine said, "Get some glasses, Piers, and we'll all have a drink." And as Piers went off to get them she looked from Linda to Sarah. "I truly am terribly sorry if you've all been worrying."

Sarah said that she had been demented, she was quite sure her mother had had an accident and was dead.

"No, Sarah, you weren't," said Linda. "Don't be so dramatic." And to her mother, "But we were getting very anxious. It was unlike you to be out so late without letting us know."

David looked at her apologetically. "I'm afraid I'm to blame, Linda. Your mother and I were at my flat and we were talking and didn't realise that time was passing."

Sarah, who was now beginning to feel very much happier, wondered how much talk had been going on. Judging from her mother's and David's shining eyes that hadn't been all they had been doing. She thought how strange it was that until her mother had said she was going to marry David she hadn't even considered the possibility of her marrying again. Which just showed how stupid she had been.

Catherine let Linda take her coat and case and sank down in a chair.

"What have you been doing this evening, Linda?"

"I had dinner with Dirk Marion. I can't imagine why I thought I didn't like him. He's awfully nice, Mother. I've asked him to dinner tomorrow night if that's all right with you."

"Of course, darling," said Catherine, delighted at this news. It struck her that Linda was looking quite different this evening. So much happier. The haunted look had gone from her eyes. It was as if a weight had been lifted from her shoulders.

"Scotch is a bit low," said Piers coming back into the room with the drinks and glasses.

"I only want a very weak one," said David, "then I must be on my way. I've got a busy day tomorrow and so I know has your mother." He held out his hand to Catherine who put hers into it. "Incidentally your mother and I have fixed the date for our wedding. A month today."

Catherine saw the relief on her three children's faces. She wondered if perhaps after all it was what they wanted? Certainly Linda and Piers looked much happier than they had at breakfast. She supposed Linda was happier because Dirk and she had had dinner together and her antagonism towards him was over. She had the impression that Linda had cleared her mind of something that had been making her unhappy since her return from New York, as if she were determining now to make a fresh start in life, to forsake the past and from now on be very much happier.

She looked at the time and was astonished to find it was nearly midnight.

"Sarah darling, off you go to bed or you'll never be up in the morning to get to *Amanda's* by half-past nine."

"I know, Mummy. I'll go off right away. Incidentally I left a note on your desk for you this evening before I went to the flicks with Harriet."

She kissed David, asked her mother to look in and say good-night to her and left the room.

"What do you imagine all that was about?" asked Linda. "How Sarah does love to be mysterious!"

Catherine went across to her desk, read the note and said it wasn't really particularly important. Obviously Linda was no more in Sarah's confidence than Sarah was in Linda's. She supposed since Linda had been in America the two sisters had grown apart. But that they were very fond of each other she didn't doubt for a moment.

"I'll be off to bed too," said Linda. "Come in and say good-night to me, Mother."

"Of course I will."

Linda went to David and kissed him. "Good-night, David, and thank you."

Piers, who had been out of the room, put his head in the door to know if he should put his mother's car in the garage or would David like to be driven home.

"Thanks, Piers, but I'll get a taxi."

"What was Linda thanking you for, darling?" asked Catherine when David and she were alone.

"I'll tell you some other time. It's a long story. At the moment I'm under a pledge of secrecy about it. I think most likely she will tell you herself. But I don't think you are going to have any need to worry any more about her. She'll probably be unhappy at times but those times will grow more and more infrequent. I have a feeling that from now on all will be well for her and I have an idea Dirk will be joining the family before long if Linda will have him and I'm pretty sure she will."

Catherine's face lit up. She too felt happier than she had for a long time.

"All three of them seem different this evening. Read this. It's the note Sarah left me."

David read it, a smile on his face. He handed it back to her.

"Linda and Sarah, that's two of your children with their problems settled."

"Thank God. I worried most about Linda because I realised hers was a really serious one but I was also very anxious about Sarah."

"I know you were, darling. Now there only remains Piers to get himself sorted out."

"It may be wishful thinking but it struck me that he too seemed happier this evening."

David drew her close to him. "I thought so too. But now — I want to see you looking better. You've had too much worry recently over your family."

"I recuperate very quickly." Catherine glanced at herself anxiously in the Chippendale mirror over the mantelpiece and saw that though her eyes were still shining she looked exhausted. As indeed she felt! It had been an emotional evening.

"David, do I look awful? Just an old hag? That's because I'm not young any more."

David bent and kissed her. "Nonsense. You could never look an old hag and to me you will always look young."

Catherine smiled. "You're terribly good for my morale, David."

"You're good for mine, too. It's been at a very low ebb recently."

They heard Piers returning from putting the car away.

"Good-night, darling," said David. "Off you go to bed and sleep well. Let's have lunch together tomorrow and then maybe in the evening I could take you all out and we'll have a family party. A more successful one I hope than your birthday one."

"I can't, David. I must be in. Linda ha asked Dirk to dinner."

"So she has. I'd forgotten."

"You come too."

David grinned. "I will and I'll arrive wit champagne. It's time we celebrated. Thes past few weeks have been far too bleak."

Catherine went to the door with him and once more he held her close and kissed her.

"Till tomorrow, Catherine."

"Till tomorrow, David."

She closed the door and locked it. Piers was putting the drinks away and collecting the glasses when she returned to the drawing-room. "Bed, Piers, we're late."

"I know." It struck Piers that though his mother was looking exhausted she was also looking happy. For which he was grateful. He had been relieved when David had said he and his mother had finally settled on a date for their wedding. He had been so afraid that it might not come off. That because of Linda, Sarah and himself his mother might have decided she couldn't give up their home and leave them. Which was absurd because it was time all three of them learned to fend for themselves. Well, perhaps not Sarah for a little while yet but it wouldn't be long before she too would want to live on her own.

"I say, Mother, I'm delighted to know David and you are being married so soon. I've been a bit worried because you hadn't said a word about any definite date, in fact since your birthday you haven't mentioned getting married."

"I know. But — well, I just couldn't make up my mind about it."

"Why not?"

"Darling, a lot of reasons."

"Linda, Sarah and me being three of them?"

"Maybe." And suddenly Catherine decided to be frank with him. After all, Piers wasn't a child any more. "I had thought till this evening I couldn't give up this house and as you and Linda didn't want to live with David and me — "

"Oh, Mother — "

"Well, that was what you both said."

"I've been terribly afraid it might have been something like that. And — ?"

"This evening I realised as I was walking across Kensington Gardens that I had been wrong. That none of you would want me to give up David for you."

"I'll say we wouldn't."

"So I went to see him and told him I wasn't going to let my family stand in our way."

"Thank God you did. We would never have forgiven ourselves if you had."

Piers looked at his mother. "You're not worrying about us any more, are you?"

"Not really. Linda seems very much happier this evening. I think that's because Dirk and she had dinner together and — I don't know for certain but I have an idea there's something in the wind there."

"And how about Sarah — ?"

"Well, she's been entangled with a married man for some weeks now but thank God that's over. I only discovered that tonight."

"Which means that I remain the only one to concern you?" Piers put his hands on her shoulders. "Mother dear, I don't think I need worry you any more either. I've some news for you. I'm going back to Lawson's."

Catherine's heart lifted. This was indeed good news.

"I'm delighted, darling. So long as you'll be happy working for them again."

"I will be, I promise you. I was a

damned fool ever to have left. It was more than I deserved to have old man Lawson agreeing to take me on again."

"How did it come about, Piers?"

"Through a girl called Jane Armstrong. I must have mentioned her to you when I was working there. She's his secretary and she told Mr. Lawson that she believed I would like to be taken on again if they would have me. Apparently he said he would and she called me up and said she had fixed an appointment and I was to keep it. Jane's very strong-minded." He smiled remembering Jane's telephone call that had come out of the blue a couple of days ago. He had believed after their last meeting that she was finally through with him. But apparently he had been mistaken. He had been surprised to find how glad he was that he had been wrong. He knew now that he had been more in love with her and she with him than he had realised. "I'd like you to meet Jane. I think you'll like her. Can I ask her to dinner one evening?"

"Of course, darling, just as soon as you like."

Catherine thought that it was a very long while since she had felt so happy. Now it would seem she had no cause for concern over any of her children.

"I'll give her a call tomorrow and tell her." Piers bent and kissed his mother. "You've been marvellous, Mother, the way you have coped with us all. I don't know what any of us has done to deserve you."

"Nonsense. I can't imagine what I would have done without you. And now — bed."

Catherine went upstairs and looked into Sarah's room to find her still awake. She bent and kissed her.

"Thank you for your note, darling."

"I hoped you'd be glad I was through with Garry."

"I am. And — next time, Sarah, don't choose a married man."

"I won't." Sarah reached up her arms and hugged her mother. "I'm terribly glad David and you are definitely getting married."

"I hoped you would be."

"I think he's super. But then I always have." Another bear-like hug. "And so are you."

"Bless you, now off you go to sleep."

Sarah lay back against her pillows. She was surprised to find that now she wasn't feeling in the least unhappy. Her mother had of course been right. Her next boy-friend would certainly not be married.

Catherine went into Linda's room. She was in bed but not reading. Just lying there looking utterly contented.

"Good-night, Linda darling. Sleep well."

Linda too reached up and put her arms round her mother's neck. "I will, Mummy, I'm certain. I'm afraid I've been hell these past few weeks since I came home but I won't be any more."

"I'm glad. I've hated to see you so unhappy."

"I'll be all right now. One day I'll tell you what happened in New York. But I'd rather not for a little while."

Catherine smoothed Linda's hair back from her forehead. "You needn't ever tell me if you don't want to."

"I'd like to. It's a tragic story. But I've already told it once today to Dirk and I couldn't bear to go through it again."

"You shan't, Linda, my darling."

"I wouldn't have told Dirk except that he knew about it. That was why he was so anxious to see me. Now it is *I* who want to see him. And I think I will quite often."

"I'm glad. I've only met him once or twice but I like him enormously."

"So do I."

Piers was just going into his room as Catherine left Linda's. He stooped and kissed her.

"Good-night, Mother, sleep well. And you might tell me in the morning what you would like for a wedding present. Linda, Sarah and I are all going to pool our resources to give you one. Remember the comic presents we used to give you when we were kids?"

Catherine did indeed. The little glass cat on her bedside table had been a present from Linda when she had been around eight. There was a bedraggled pin cushion that Sarah had laboriously made for her at her nursery school and a framed water colour of a ship in a rough sea that Piers had painted when he had reached his teens.

"Of course I remember them. I have them all."

Piers grinned. "My sentimental old Mum! But this time we will give you something worth keeping. I hope you will want me to give you away. I assure you I will to David with my blessing."

This book is published under the auspices of the

ULVERSCROFT FOUNDATION,

a registered charity, whose primary object is to assist those who experience difficulty in reading print of normal size.

In response to approaches from the medical world, the Foundation is also helping to purchase the latest, most sophisticated medical equipment desperately needed by major eye hospitals for the diagnosis and treatment of eye diseases.

If you would like to know more about the

ULVERSCROFT FOUNDATION,

and how you can help to further its work, please write for details to:

THE ULVERSCROFT FOUNDATION
The Green, Bradgate Road
Anstey
Leicestershire
England

We hope this Large Print edition gives you the pleasure and enjoyment we ourselves experienced in its publication.

There are now 1,000 titles available in this ULVERSCROFT Large Print Series. Ask to see a Selection at your nearest library.

The Publisher will be delighted to send you, free of charge, upon request a complete and up-to-date list of all titles available.

Ulverscroft Large Print Books Ltd.
The Green, Bradgate Road
Anstey, Leicester
England